I wasn't searching for a fight with ̲ *and
bone. The full-grown Doberman has* ̲ *if he goes for
your throat it's hopeless. I'd seen one* ̲ *trying to make for the
Wall in East Berlin. There are mines and the Vopos have automatic
rifles, but it was the Doberman that got him. You have to be suicidal
to try and hop the Wall, and it's not much better going any other way.
I know. I've been.*

Introducing Cody, whose first appearance on the spy fiction scene
in 1979 had the reviewers drooling on both sides of the Atlantic:

- "Well written and thoroughly gripping" (Glasgow Herald);
- "New, original, fashionably tense" (The Listener);
- "Sophisticated spy-fi...full of promise" (The Guardian);
- "(Brierley) has the skill and originality to inject freshness at
  every level" (Tribune);
- "Full of action and expertise" (Observer);
- "This tough-minded woman is a perfect heroine" (New York
  Times Book Review);
- "A good, fast, tight thriller" (Newsday);
- "A splendid thriller" (St Louis Post-Dispatch);
- "Tough...witty...in the best tradition of suspense fiction" (New
  Yorker).

*David Brierley was born in 1936 in Durban and has lived in South
Africa, Canada, Greece and England, though currently resides in
France. He has worked as a wholesale salesman, teacher in a French
school, advertising copywriter and then as a full time writer. He has
written numerous travel articles and twelve novels which have been
set in France, Holland, Germany, Poland, Czechoslovakia, Hungary,
Romania, Tunisia, El Salvador, Brazil and Bolivia. This has meant
research trips where he has been able to indulge his passion for
travel. He hates talking about himself, but when the first 'Cody' books
appeared, the* Whodunit Guide to Crime, Suspense and Spy Fiction
(1982) *noted that they "showed a mind of considerable intelligence,
sharp observation of contemporary mores in Europe and Britain and
something of the early Le Carre mould".*

Top Notch Thrillers

Ostara Publishing's imprint **Top Notch Thrillers** aims to revive Great British thrillers which do not deserve to be forgotten. Each title has been carefully selected not just for its plot or sense of adventure, but for the distinctiveness and sheer quality of its writing.

COLD WAR

DAVID BRIERLEY

Ostara Publishing

First published in 1979

Copyright © David Brierley 1979

ISBN 978 1906288 617

A CIP reference is available from the British Library

Printed and Bound in the United Kingdom

Ostara Publishing
13 King Coel Road
Colchester
CO3 9AG
www.ostarapublishing.co.uk

The Series Editor for Top Notch Thrillers is Mike Ripley, author of the award-winning 'Angel' comic thrillers, co-editor of the three *Fresh Blood* anthologies promoting new British crime writing and, for ten years, the crime fiction critic of the *Daily Telegraph*. He currently writes the 'Getting Away With Murder' column for the e-zine *Shots* on www.shotsmag.co.uk.

For Caroline
with love and thanks

AUTHOR'S NOTE

One of the odd things about a writer's life is the way a book takes on an existence of its own after the manuscript is out of the author's hands. The editor has her/his say, the copy editor slips in corrections, even the jacket designer has opinions. Then the book is set, goes to the printer and the presses roll. The end.

But sometimes it isn't.

Faber & Faber published this edition in 1979. When Scribners in New York decided to buy it they insisted on certain changes. Cody had to have her identity changed. I wasn't privy to their reasoning but I imagine that editorial conferences are the same as meetings at any company: everyone feels they must contribute or they are not earning their salary. Someone said: 'Hey, wouldn't it be neat if we made her British?' Rosemary Goad, my editor at Faber, asked me to come to London so we could chat. I could see from her face that she was apprehensive about how I would react. Authors can have tantrums and stamp their feet. I know I have but not this time. I made the change.

This, however, is the first edition just as Faber published it. When Collins republished the book Cody had become British and so she remained through all five Cody novels.

If I could ask her, I wonder what Cody's feelings were about changing her passport.

- *David Brierley, October 2011.*

In letting of blood three main circumstances are to be considered,
who, how much, when.

ROBERT BURTON, *The Anatomy of Melancholy*

1

And then he turned in bed and said to me: "What's your name?"

I said: "Cody."

And he said: "I know that. I meant your first name."

It felt, suddenly, colder in the room.

I looked at him, not answering; looked at the blackened right eye, the bruising and lacerations and purple stains on his cheek, the stubble on his chin, an arm wrapped tightly in white, a leg in plaster. That was all I could see of him. There was the smell, behind the obvious one, a hint of the sharp smell of blood. His? And that indefinable throb of a hospital, the great bureaucratic humming machine, like an ocean liner when you go down below the public rooms, below the cabins, below the kitchens, down below right into the cold rooms with the sheep and pigs and cattle slung up from hooks. The hospital had that aura of bodies, some dead, some dying. Because we're all dying, from the day we're born.

"Does it matter?"

He thought about it a bit and said, "Thanks anyway for saving my life." It wasn't spoken easily. The voice was tired, bruised. He spoke softly, as if the crashing like a roadripper inside his skull was all the noise he could take.

It was impossible for me to tell anything of the man. We rely on intonation and eye movement and facial expression and body language, and these pointers were denied me. I judged him thirty-four or thirty-five years old; but there was something, a wariness, that said the years hadn't all been easy.

I didn't want to ask the question because I feared the answer. It required an effort of will. "How did you know my name was Cody?"

He swallowed and it pained him. "I meant it to be a lot more subtle than this. I was watching, choosing my time. Thing is, they were watching and I never knew. I'd never have known anything more if you..."

"How?" I didn't want any more thanks. My face must have looked sharper and I saw some flicker of memory blow across his eyes.

"I was careless...watching the entrance to your building. I'd seen you go out and I was waiting till you came back...make sure you were alone....Of course, I couldn't check there was no one left up in your apartment...That was a risk, we all have to take risks some time, but I didn't know they were following me; or was it you they were watching?"

His voice trailed away, mind wandering, and it was heading towards an area of dark shadows and chill. I watched his eyes lose focus on me and track across the ceiling of the hospital room. White-painted, antiseptic, impersonal. There were no flowers, no grapes, no paperback books with curling covers and promises of thrills where, for all the broken bodies and blood, you're never convinced of the existence of pain. *AGATE Samuel Henri. Salle P243* typed on a green card on the door. That was all I knew of him, except I'd saved his life. *Henri* could have been a French mistyping; he sounded American enough.

Coming back to my apartment in the Sixth arrondissement, quarter kilo of ground coffee, blue packet of cubed sugar, and Agate had stepped...

Ugly memory.

I shook my head. My own mind was wandering.

I insisted: "How did you know my name?"

His eyes refocused and again there was the pain as he swallowed.

"I never knew your first name. When someone's saved your life it's good to..."

"Call me Cody." Jesus, what had they given him? There was the drip bottle, colourless liquid, tube disappearing under the white covers. Agate had lost blood. He'd lost a lot of it fifteen metres from the entrance to my apartment building, right there on the road, stepping out, not turning to look, never seeing the car as it approached from boulevard St-Michel, accelerating, not using its horn, not braking, and...

I had to concentrate, block out the dark of my memory.

There was the noise of a door banging down the hospital corridor and a woman's scream. It went sliding into a high-pitched giggle. Doctor walked up behind one of the nurses?

"Where did you hear about me?" I had the urge to shout at him. I leaned forward, willing his mind back to me. "It's important."

"I was working in the embassy at Ankara. Last September in Turkey, you remember?"

If only I could forget. I said nothing.

"I had one of the core offices. You know how the embassy works?"

He was using shorthand, a form of code. The offices at the core of most US embassies are protected in a way that even the ambassador's own office seldom is. They are interior, no windows on the outside world. That means there is never any risk of visual surveillance. Also, there is no danger of sound snooping. With a window on an outside wall there is always the risk of a directional gun-microphone picking up sound. Even when the window is locked, a laser trained on the glass picks up the vibrations of voices inside the room and transmits them back along the beam. Somebody could be eavesdropping in complete safety in a building a couple of kilometres away. But the core offices are totally secure from outside interference.

If Agate had been at Ankara, his job was important. The embassy here is particularly sensitive: the centre of the Intelligence network that stretches from Libya in the west, through the crescent of Arab countries, Israel, Lebanon, Cyprus, Turkey itself, north to the Soviet republics bordering the Black Sea where the nuclear missile silos were.

That was why Agate was using "core offices" as a form of code, like others say, "I work for the Company." If you knew, you understood what his job entailed. I knew.

"I understand the layout," I told him.

"There was this mention of your name, talk of what you'd done when they'd tried to kill the Turkish President."

"I don't want to hear that."

"But it was always just Cody, nobody ever..."

It was no good. He'd never get to the point under his own volition.

"Listen, were you coming to see me?"

"Yes."

"Is it a run-on from that business?"

"No. That was just how I learned your name, that you lived in Paris."

There'd been a tightness in my chest which I hadn't been aware of until it eased. I found I had been holding my breath. I don't work for them. You'd never get me inside a core office. But I had been used in Turkey, tricked, moral blackmail; I don't know the

9

right expression and I didn't want to spend time thinking of it.
never wanted to think of it again.

"All right, we'll move on to this. Is it very important?"

"Important?" Agate closed his eyes briefly. "Is what important?

It was impossible. I wanted to shake him, rearrange the brain
cells and make new nerve connections until he was coherent
There had been something about the noise of the car in the narrow
street. Cars didn't accelerate like that because of the parked
vehicles and the women with their nylon shopping bags of leeks
and *biftecks* and Normandy butter and the men coming out of the
Café Charlot with another *ballon de rouge* under their belts, and
I had turned to the sound and he had shouted something, i
could have been my name or it could have been "Oh", and...

The same fragment of memory ran over and over like a film clip
in a Movieola. But I couldn't edit out the bad bits.

"Did you want to tell me something? Did you have something
to tell about Turkey?"

The human eyelid weighs on average seven grammes. His
weighed a couple of kilos.

"I'm not at Ankara any more. They moved me to Paris. And I'd
hardly got my feet under the desk when they called me in and
said this was the way it was. And if I didn't like it, that was too
damn bad. The scenario was final, there'd be no rewrites."

He spoke meaningless words. Were they feeding him
hallucinogens?

His eyes were closing.

"Don't go to sleep."

In the street I had seen him, so intent on reaching me, eyes
on my face, even raising a hand, and I'd shouted a warning about
the car and he'd become aware of it for the first time and tried to
jump. He'd escaped the worst. He hadn't gone under the wheels
red paintbrush of death. One wing had caught him, discarded
him like a Raggedy Andy at the edge of the road, where he'd
landed at the feet of an old boy in a beret, Gauloise staining his
moustache yellow, *baguette* under his arm. They still have them
in France, looking like they've wandered out of some Fernandel
movie of a vanished bucolic past.

"*Eh, le salopard.*"

It wouldn't have mattered so much if a Citroen 2CV had clipped
Agate, but it had been a Porsche and they're solid.

The car hadn't stopped.

"I argued," Agate said. "It seemed..."

10

His voice was growing exhausted. I leaned closer.

"It was unbearable."

"What is it?" I asked.

"It was too much. The whole game seemed suddenly immoral, know what I mean?"

There was a brief spark in his eyes, appealing to me. It died.

Seemed suddenly immoral? I don't know what the Agency is meant to be about, and I don't think anyone else does. Destabilizing, infiltrating, disinformation, buying and selling foreign politicians like they were packs of detergents. Is that what fills the agendas at all the subcommittee meetings they have at Langley? But I didn't say anything. Agate had thought the Agency had a moral purpose and maybe that made him an idealist or a fool, and in either case it was surprising they had recruited him.

"You've got to believe me, it's nothing to do with Turkey. It's just I was working there with Duraine when McKosker was sent to clean up. And then they were both here in Paris. I hadn't known that. I just went into this room and they were sitting there, hanging-judge look in their eyes...It was too much...I went missing, three days, four days. I didn't go back to my apartment...Stayed at the Hotel Select, just off...Then I remembered you...There was nobody else I could trust."

He stopped. He was looking at me, but frowning, puzzled.

"What is it?" If I could put the right note of authority into my voice it might pull him back. Might.

Perhaps he didn't want to tell. Perhaps he couldn't. It depended how severe his training had been. Counter Interrogation Techniques were frightening in their logic now. For those in high-risk positions it was no longer a question of familiarization with bright lights and the effects of the major drug groups and of raising the pain threshold through rehearsal. The programme had been put together by psychologists at the Defence Department.

"Tell me."

In common humanity they should tattoo it under the left nipple: *I cannot talk*. When the psychologists bring out their jargon and pronounce a man "stress-processed", what they mean is that he is incapable of answering questions.

His conscious brain slips, shying away from the big thing, imprinted behaviour patterns taking over. He would react to the stimulus of pain by an automatic response of trivialities, touching the subject but avoiding the important heart. Stimulus: pain. Response: trivialities. Trivialities rather than silence because

part of the technique is that the person being interrogated should
believe he is cooperating. Intensify stimulus: reinforce response
And so it goes.

The clever psychologists have completely rewritten the grammar
of interrogation. But they have neglected to tell the torturers. Or
the torturers, with a hunger that has to be fed, have elected not
to believe.

In Agate's case there were the trivialities about staying at the
Hotel Select and being in Ankara with Duraine and McKosker
He thought he was cooperating and was puzzled that I kept on at
him.

The technique isn't one hundred per cent successful, because
the raw material is human. But when it works it is no good applying
greater and greater pain. Pain was the stimulus and it led to the
ultimate reward: unconsciousness, oblivion; pain providing its
own anaesthetic when it became intolerable.

"Agate."

He was associating me with the pain inflicted when the Porsche
bumped him. In his confused brain I was now the pain-stimulus

"Is it a mission? Here?"

"I didn't know they'd try and kill me. I forgot the kerb-drill
learned..."

His eyes closed again. He was breathing slowly.

"Agate, look at me. Do you mean Duraine and McKosker were
in the car?"

He felt threatened in this environment. Out of it I might have
been able to transfer my will inside him.

"Agate, is it an Intelligence operation? Is there a defector? Is
there a defence scandal? Is it the election?"

Negative. I'd hoped for involuntary reaction.

"Such dirty..."

He turned his face away. He couldn't look at me any more.
was constant pain. He had wanted to see me and now he couldn't
bear to turn his eyes in my direction.

And then the little nurse came in, as flat and sterile as Evian
water.

"I said only ten minutes." Her eyes went from me to the patient
in bed. *"Ah bon Dieu, qu'est-ce que c'est passé?"*

I'd learn no more from Agate that day.

I decided he was delirious. Blood loss, shock, drugs. Fantasies
of plots and threats on his life.

I walked down the steps from the hospital and on to the boulevard Victor Hugo and then I stopped. No, he wasn't delirious. My mind went back to that morning.

He'd raised his hand as I had turned and shouted and the Porsche had made its point and driven on and the old man in the beret had muttered, *"Eh bien, pas de numéro d'immatriculation."* Not quite true. But the number plate was as obscured by mud as a farm tractor's.

That was one thing. It was an untraceable murder vehicle.

It was the other thing that clinched it.

I hadn't telephoned. It would have been somebody from the Café Charlot or the dry cleaners or Madame Boyer with her window on the world and nothing better to occupy herself.

I had waited, holding my packages, trying to understand what the look on his face had meant. It had held something of both hope and despair.

The ambulance was there before the police and that wasn't like Paris. There was a small crowd of the morbid growing bigger and the ambulanceman had felt a pulse and they put Agate on a stretcher and almost got him in the ambulance before the hoo-ha bragged its way down the street. They had to leave the police car at the corner because of the jam and that didn't improve their tempers. Two of Paris's finest, one with his hand drawing strength from lying on his pistol holster. The cops thrust their faces into the back of the ambulance.

"Eh attendez, pas si vite."

"Qu'est-ce qu'il y a?"

"C'est un bercy?"

"Non, pas saoul. Il était fatigué de vivre, je pense."

Then a lot more police arrived and began pushing people in the chest and shouting and asking Algerians for their papers and boosting their egos.

Routine. Not that.

The thing was they'd taken Agate all the way to the American hospital in Neuilly.

Perhaps they looked for his papers in the ambulance and found he was an American. Perhaps. They certainly hadn't looked while he was bleeding in the gutter. It was a long way to take an emergency to Neuilly.

The inference, and it was strong, was that the accident was no accident: they knew him, had been waiting a couple of blocks away, anticipating the impact, hoping to clear off with the body.

13

When the police had caught them they had driven to the American hospital because they knew he was American.

I walked slowly again. If it were like that, they'd be watching now at the hospital entrance.

I swung round.

There was a man wearing a cap and overalls with a kiosk and buckets of carnations, blue and yellow irises, roses with no scent. A man with a table laid with copies of the *Herald-Tribune*, *Time*, *Newsweek*, *Playboy*. Taxis, with drivers smoking and staring. Usual cop. Usual cars passing. Cars stopped. Two men were coming out of the hospital entrance behind me.

Walk slowly and were they staring because I had been with Agate or because I'm a woman?

Think about that and be careful crossing the street.

2

Others would have knocked.

I looked at the door and wondered why.

It came again. The fist used as a hammer.

When I opened the door, they came through like a crowd leaving a factory gate, three of them in uniform and one in a belted fawn raincoat. None of them had a gun out, but their eyes flicked round the room searching for an excuse. The uniformed men opened doors into my bedroom, the bathroom, the kitchen and the closet while the man in the belted raincoat stood next to me, quite still. There was no embarrassment in him. There never is.

Language hadn't been invented.

The uniformed men came back into the living room and shook their heads. The room seemed full of them. It's a gift they have.

"You're not armed?" the man in the raincoat asked. It was half appeal, half question. There were streaks of wet on the shoulders and back of the coat. It was raining again.

I said nothing.

"I mean, you don't have a gun hidden on you?" There was an accent there but it wasn't heavy enough to get him any speaking parts for Frenchmen in Hollywood. His eyes travelled north to south over my body and back again. "No, I don't think there's any

14

gun." He waved a hand at the uniformed men. *"Alors, attendez en dehors."*

The men were gone. They were not only tough and thorough, but quick and sharp. When the door had closed he said, "My name is Crevecoeur." He made a deprecatory smile. "A thousand apologies about the name, which I was born with, but it has turned out appropriate for someone in my occupation."

I didn't ask.

"I am a Chief Inspector in the SN."

It was a little joke, said with the smoothness of practice.

In the silence I thought I saw a trace of a shadow cross his face at my lack of reaction.

"The Sûreté Nationale, you understand."

"Yes, I know. You gave me my *carte de séjour*." I didn't intend it to sound as if he'd stamped it personally, but Crevecoeur brought out the deprecatory smile again.

"One of our tasks, helping foreigners with their residence papers."

"Since you've forced your way in here..."

"No force." He was quick with that. "You opened the door to us."

"I'd like to see your card."

He dug out a wallet and flipped it open to show the card and photo under the yellowing plastic. I didn't bother.

"It's easy to get these things."

It was hard to tell if he was angry and trying to hide it, or not angry but wanting to impress.

"You're mistaken. It's damn hard. It's taken me eighteen years to get here. There are examinations to pass. There is a lot of competition. You have to work hard. There is the constant danger from armed criminals."

Crevecoeur had a long face with vertical creases between the eyebrows and down the cheeks and in the cleft of the chin, as if he'd got his head through a door once and the villains on the far side had put their shoulders to it and shoved hard to close it.

He took off his raincoat and I thought it was to settle himself in. But he undid the two buttons on his shirt just above the belt and there was a long scar, too high up for an appendectomy.

"1971, Marseille, North African with a knife. He had a suitcase full of *kif*."

He pushed back his left sleeve and there was the purple knot of an old bullet wound.

"1974, Orly airport, attempted hijacking. You might remember the case. One of my men was killed, I was in hospital, and the man who did it went free. A Palestinian. Our government contacted Gaddafi, and a Libyan Air Force Mirage flew the gentleman out the next day. His career finally ended a Mogadishu. One grows weary of the politicians saying they know what is best for France."

And I thought: this one would hide his actions from the politicians. It would be a principle.

He parted the hair behind his left ear.

"1976, Café Flore. Again you may recall it from the newspapers A prominent lawyer was killed in the confusion. It was a vendetta between the Corsican gang..."

"All right." I held up a hand.

The window was closed against the weather but sounds of the early evening rush hour drifted in. It was no different from the morning rush hour or the midday rush hour except the drivers had spent all their patience during the day and were running on their nerves. It gets a little worse each year, but the young ones think that is progress and the old ones blame the government.

"Why do you include me in such company?"

Crevecoeur got out a pack of Gitanes, offered them and lit one himself. "You don't mind..." he asked after it was alight. "Would you like to make some coffee?"

"Not particularly."

"I'd like coffee. It's been a difficult day. Or perhaps whisky."

"Listen, is this a social call?"

"Mademoiselle Cody, you are a friend of Mr Agate?"

"No."

"But you went to the hospital."

"A hit and run driver got him this morning," I nodded at the window. "He was crossing the street to speak to me. I felt partially responsible and got a taxi to follow the ambulance."

"Why did he want to speak with you?"

"I don't know."

"You were with him, alone in a private room, for ten minutes.

There was no ashtray. Crevecoeur had a vague way of looking round that had nothing to do with being a policeman but everything to do with concentrating on more important things. He tapped the cigarette ash into his cupped hand. There was a spark, briefly in his palm and it died. He walked over, opened the window and blew the ash out. He stared down at the street.

16

"I see the boys from the quai des Orfèvres have been busy, making pictures on the road with their chalk. That's what the book tells them to do." He sighed. "Wasting their time. The chalk will wash away in the rain long before the blood." He drew on the cigarette, letting the smoke drift up. "Don't let me talking stop you. You were going to make coffee."

He followed into the kitchen and had to keep moving out of the way as I got out coffee, filters, cups and filled the kettle with water.

"I'm glad you don't use instant coffee. I was afraid, being American..."

"You don't like Americans?"

"On the contrary. Some of my best friends are American." There seemed no trace of irony in his voice. Perhaps the phrase didn't have overtones to a Frenchman.

He was letting the talk die. Perhaps he was waiting for me to step out of line and confess Agate was my lover and I'd pushed him under the car in a fit of jealousy. So we played poker while the kettle boiled and the coffee dripped but I tired of it first and prompted him.

"You're not concerned about a hit and run driver."

"No. I'm interested in you and why Agate wanted to speak to you."

"All right, now you've seen me. I know nothing about Agate, except he is careless crossing the street. I have lived here eighteen months, learning the language, travelling a little, living my life. And Agate has no part of that life, none."

"Good coffee. When I was in America I found the coffee weak."

"You were on holiday?"

"No."

It was such a final negative. That "no" was going to give nothing away, which meant that it did. If you don't visit another country on holiday, there's only one other reason.

He knew I'd be working it out and his eyes searched for hints of nervousness or deception.

"You haven't told me all about yourself," he went on.

"Who does?"

"Come, you know what I'm referring to."

The oldest trick in the book, implying total knowledge so that the other person relaxes and gives something away. I made a noncommittal face.

"We don't have a dossier on you," Crevecoeur said. "At least,

17

until today. Your application for residence is on file, of course. haven't contacted the tax people yet."

"I'm not working here."

"You're living here." He looked round in his deceptive vague way. "Very pleasant. It's not American luxury, but any apartment in the centre of Paris is expensive. You need money."

"It comes from America. A legacy." A fiction, but it does.

"You must still do your work with the tax form and lie like everybody else." He put his long face on one side to look at me. "We need to know everything is in order when you apply for renewal of your *carte de séjour.*"

Message received.

Eighteen months and they'd never bothered me, until now. Until a frightened man with four days' stubble on his chin had tried to speak to me and became a traffic statistic.

"For instance," he continued, "we'll need evidence that the money really has been transferred from America and not earned here in some discreet way. Because discreet ways can be very indiscreet." The furrow between his eyes said: We know all about Agate but we're not certain about you. "And legacy or not, there must be evidence that the money has been declared for tax purposes in the United States or in France. Do I make myself clear?"

Perfectly. The thing was to treat him like a dog. Show no fear or irritation, because they can smell that. I kept still.

"Good." He rubbed his eyes with his knuckles. "A bloody difficult day. And this is going to be the most bloody difficult part of it. have to question you but without putting direct questions. It happens in security matters. I cannot ask Do you know this man, Have you heard this thing. And you said getting a Chief Inspector's card was easy. I don't want to take you to my office. Some people it impresses, but others it paralyses. They are frightened they'll meet men with big sticks. I don't know how the idea gets around."

"You must have been out at the time."

"Possibly."

He put down his cup, stepped close. I had to repress the desire to move back and it was nothing to do with the woman/man dimension. We all have to preserve that territory near us. It's an animal instinct that makes people keep their distance, except a child or a lover, whom we allow close for protection.

"In America they place reliance on polygraph machines, lie detectors. We have the best lie detector in the world present in

18

this room. The human face. The size of the pupils, the direction of gaze, the jaw muscles, the plane of the cheeks beside the mouth, the skin under the eyes, the vertical contractions between the eyebrows, the perspiration glands on the forehead, the skin tones. But you would know all this, wouldn't you?"

Implying full knowledge of my background and training. Trying his luck to see if I reacted. Ignore.

He was staring in my face, concentrating, very close. I could smell the tobacco on his breath.

"We will play a game. I'll say a phrase and I want you, without hesitation, to say what comes in your mind. I want instant free association. Do you understand?"

"Understood."

Let him play his games. I knew nothing about Agate, his fears, his enemies. I didn't understand why Sûreté Nationale was here. I was ignorant. I had nothing to hide, to lie about.

"President."

"Carter."

"President." He repeated it, voice unemotional.

"Giscard."

"Dentist."

"Toothache."

"Atom bomb."

"Hiroshima."

"Siberia."

"Ivan Denisovich."

"Beach."

"Dog."

It broke the flow and I saw a tremble in his left eyelid and then a slight upturn of his lips as he worked out the implied pun on his accent. He was good but he would never have taken me in serious interrogation if I could break his control over the flow of questions like that.

"Omaha."

"Invasion."

"Mirage."

"Jet fighter."

His eyes took in the whole of my face but never moved. Only that eyelid wasn't steady.

"Black."

"Shirt."

"Cold War."

19

"Soviet Union."

"*Arc de Triomphe.*"

"Horse race."

"*Quatorze juillet.*"

"*La Bastille.*"

"*Ladouceur.*"

"Softness."

"Orange."

"Holland."

"Blood."

"Red."

"Time."

"To stop."

No, he wouldn't have taken me. I'd already seen his tension ease and the eyelid stop after the key phrase had been slipped in somewhere and I hadn't reacted. The lie detector of the face works both ways.

He nodded and turned, a little smile round the eyes, making for the living room. He looked round again as he put on his raincoat, no longer seeing the place in terms of menace.

"It's a good room. Discs, books, desk, you spend time on your own. Much better than some of the places I have to go into."

His eyes flicked round suddenly to catch the look on my face.

"You've shown no curiosity why I came."

"I've done nothing," I said. "I don't want to become involved. It's your affair not mine."

He was reluctant to give me up. Whatever it was, he considered it important enough to come out on a rain-filled afternoon in November. He was wary of me, couldn't accept I was unconnected.

"Do you take sleeping pills?"

"I try not to. I sleep badly. I'm afraid of becoming dependent." Also, during drug-induced sleep the brain's perception of smells and sounds is dulled. I value my life and cannot allow that; but it was no concern of his.

"Chloral hydrate?"

He was belting the raincoat, and looked up. I made a little negative movement. He kept searching my face and I kept telling myself: Don't think about it, don't get involved.

"Agate had a drip bottle," he said. "You saw?"

"Yes."

"It was a saline drip. Do you have any medical knowledge?"

"If I have a headache, I take an aspirin. Anything worse, I see

20

he doctor." Why should I tell him? They always think your life is heir property.

"I was forgetting. We French are a nation of hypochondriacs, ve all think we know about medicine. When I saw Agate, I asked he doctor about the bottle and he said it was an isotonic saline solution—that is, it can be mixed with the body fluids without :ausing imbalance. Nine grammes of sodium chloride to one litre »f water, that's what he told me. There was a lot of other nformation I didn't understand. Osmotic pressure?" He shrugged.

I waited for it. My brain said: Don't think, don't get involved. 3ut my stomach already knew.

"Somebody had introduced chloral hydrate into the drip bottle. 'm waiting on the pathologist's report, but it must have been a nassive dose. You would have noticed the effects even while you vere with him. The pulse grows feebler, difficulty in breathing, coma, leath. Agate probably died while you were crossing the boulevard /ictor Hugo. You see, you are involved. You had been in his room."

There was a gust of wind and the rain came tapping at the vindow, wanting to come in. Crevecoeur was waiting. His was a ob that required patience.

"You thought it might be me?" I asked.

"Not really. It was probably put in the drip bottle half an hour »efore you saw him. But..." He had a final vague look round the 'oom as though he'd overlooked a clue. "But I can't decide whether omeone wanted us to believe it was you, or whether it was :hance. I suppose you can't help?"

I could think of nothing to say. I was too busy keeping the urmoil from showing in my face. Would Duraine murder one of iis own people? Would he try and implicate me? The answers veren't comforting.

Crevecoeur looked at the window and sighed. Rivulets of water 'an down the pane.

"Thank you for the coffee." He opened the door to the landing ind said, "You won't see me again. Unless there is some trouble ibout your *carte de séjour*. If I may give you one piece of advice, it s what I always say to a woman: it would be better if you forgot ill about me."

Another little joke, worn smooth with practice.

In a moment there were voices in the street below. I saw Crevecoeur walking with the three uniformed men. He was turning ip the collar of his raincoat. They wouldn't walk far, not the Sûreté. The car would be round the corner. Discreet.

21

3

I kill, therefore I am.

Descartes would cry for the twentieth century.

Look in the eyes, in the dark of the eyes, and that's the philosophy you see there.

They were swift. The first time they tried to kill me was that same evening. I don't know how many there were. Five, six, more There could have been twenty, forty, a hundred. I didn't know the resources of their organization. I didn't know what their organization was. I didn't know why they wanted to kill me. All knew was that I had become contaminated, vermin to be shot.

If you want to kill somebody in France, an election is the perfect time, a political rally the ideal location.

Shoot someone at his front door, post him a bomb, push him under the métro, slip ground glass in his coffee, anything, and the police mentality checks enemies, motives, alibis for the night of the eighteenth, the usual. Perhaps they run up a blind alley, perhaps they run up against a blind magistrate, but they're trying. The newspapers are sniffing because the presses run better on blood

But French elections exist in an ill-defined area between individual chaos and ritualized violence. The banners are direct Death to the Reds, Fascist Assassins, *Giscard au poteau*. The speaker's mouth moves but that is unimportant: only his fist in the air has meaning. In the crowd are fifty or a hundred other speakers, each his own storm centre, nucleus of violent emotion

The police are down the side streets—still, silent, waiting, waiting. They hold batons and have lead weights in the hems of their capes.

When Authority judges it time to show its power, the CRS come in their snub-nosed Berliet trucks. The riot police: because that is what they provoke. They are the victors of every election.

No political rally is successful without broken heads, blood flowing down faces, ribs fractured as the bodies lie in the gutter and the boot goes in.

If a body is found lifeless, the rally is explanation enough.

The newspapers carry smudgy photos of people running, placards heaped and burning, a snapshot of the dead one from the family album. The front page carries skyscrapers of headlines, so many it's unnecessary to read the story: The biggest blackest screamer: *UN MORT, 23 BLESSÉS.* One dead, twenty-three wounded.

I was the one.

It was ten days to the election. President Giscard would lose. Everybody said so.

I saw five of them, but there'd be others I didn't see. These were the field operatives and they'd have directors and analysts, the people who filled out forms in triplicate at the armoury door and the people who queried expenses, all the others with soft jobs at the control office. It wasn't some private little war I'd got caught up in. Besides, they didn't look like the 20,000-franc contract boys from the Ninth. They dressed the same, but the gunboys have grey skin with pores that are never clean of smoke and cellar dust and 3 a.m.

They were so careless it wasn't until fifteen seconds before the end I realized they were being clever.

It was the first attempt to kill me. They'd got Agate at the second go.

I had no warning. The game without rules.

What had Agate tried to tell me? What was so important that he'd been killed?

First there was the man standing under the lamp as I left my apartment and turned down rue St-André-des-Arts. He had his head behind *Le Monde* and that was a nice touch, brought a hint of culture to it. Eight in the evening. The rain had paused, leaving the streets glistening, pools of white reflected from windows and lamps. As I passed he half-closed the paper and the face that followed me wore dark glasses. It was the dark glasses that triggered me. People wear them at night in Paris, but when it is someone standing under a lamp with a newspaper blocking half the face, it registers.

Even then I mightn't have taken him as special if I hadn't been on edge from Crevecoeur's questions. His secretiveness had been getting at me.

I decided to draw him and he took the bait, and so that was it. I had become interesting.

Why?

I crossed the road, checking for traffic, and he was forty metres behind. He took an interest in a dusty window with white enamel sinks and bidets. He still carried the newspaper, didn't use it to break the profile of his face. He held it with his hands clasped by the seat of his pants like a cousin of royalty on a factory visit. The paper wagged gently.

There was a Yamaha 250 cc down the street, engine suffering from oxygen starvation, distinctive when it idled, with a sudden puff of smoke as it exploded tk-tk-tk-bang. Two types were watching; late twenties, blue jeans, one in a black leather jacket, the other in a cast-off para's combat blouson, helmets, goggles. It was the standard uniform for tearaways, bank robbers, despatch messengers.

They were drawing attention to themselves, and I thought: Careless. But it was me.

I made a right turn and the engine note changed as it got more throttle.

Left turn and the motorbike was behind. He was an ace rider, keeping the machine at walking speed without front wheel waver.

I dismissed the idea they were Crevecoeur's men. The Sûreté might put a tail on me because I had been with Agate just before he died, but not three, not making it open.

Could there be any other reason for dogging my heels? No, the connection had to be Agate.

Left again and I was heading down towards place St-Michel. There was a gust of icy wind and I thought they were running the fountains; but it wasn't spray I saw in the street lights: the clouds had opened again.

They were holding the dress rehearsal for the revolution in the rain. Something like the United Group of the International Militant Left had taken over the square, the Left spawning united groups like a log spits out sawdust. Sociology second years from Nanterre, printers from *l'Huma*, daughters of biscuit manufacturers, *pions* from the Lycée Henri Quatre, railwaymen, refugees from Mitterand's Socialist Party, bookshop assistants, tourists from Amsterdam caught up in the excitement, market porters, the out-of-work, the never-work. They knew what they were against: they were against the world. When they tried to agree what they were for, they'd split again.

The noise. You could disguise a lot in that noise. There were protests from cars caught in the unexpected jam, a man in a black raincoat gripping a mike plugged into a van with amplifier and loudspeaker, arguments among the crowd, face to face, angry, mouths working but not ears, a young woman in a brilliant red track suit with a face ecstatic at her own torrent of rhetoric, hair slicked by rain, cheeks gleaming as if from tears.

The man with the mike punched the exhaust fumes out of the rain.

"...destroyed our freedom, our youth brutalized in the army, our old thrown on the dung-hill of neglect, while in Africa French arms are sent to murder..."

The Yamaha was steady behind.

An unfriendly party could get knife-close in the maelstrom and away again and nobody would understand the cry wasn't one of anger. There would be a headline in the morning newspaper but the story would tell nothing.

No one ever explained what Tixier-Belfort had been doing in the march down boulevard Haussman, but there he was lying in his own blood outside Marks et Spencer. He made a headline in the late editions: *Mystery death of famous defence lawyer*. The paper carried a picture of the widow and fifteen-year-old daughter.

The alternatives were dwindling and I still hadn't seen they were trying to be clever, making the tail obvious. They probably had others waiting if I'd tried other options on the way.

Left again, back into rue St-André-des-Arts.

What they were doing was this: they were running me like a pack of African wild dogs run an antelope, always one ahead of the pack, turning the animal, never letting it rest, until it comes to the lip of the *kloof* with the hundred-metre drop and turns, exhausted, to face a dozen open jaws.

The VW Beetle pulled out, passed me, stopped eighty metres in front. It was an anonymous car, 59 on the number plate, registered in the Nord. As I moved closer I caught a glimpse of the face reflected in the door mirror, of pale skin and shadowed eyes.

The Yamaha turned into the street behind, then idled, the tk-tk-tk-bang audible above the crowd noise from the square.

There was one street, more an alley, turning right and running down to quai des Grands Augustins along the Seine.

I took it and the throttle on the Yamaha said I was being followed.

The bread van occupied the road in front, its back doors gaping, the man loading a half-basket with long loaves.

I was running now as the man turned. His white coat was

unbuttoned, leather jacket bulky underneath, and one of the long loaves caught the light from an uncurtained window and glinted metal.

The Yamaha was behind me, insistent.

One option left.

Rue de l'Hirondelle, narrower still, cul-de-sac for cars, but steps and a passage back into place St-Michel. I could hear the orator, voice distorted by shouting into the microphone, the crowd responding to the sweep of his voice, the emotion, the repetitions, the old tricks.

"...because we are the people, we are the power, we are the future, we are the tide that sweeps away the flotsam on the beach, irresistible, cleansing away the bourgeois scum, saluting the new dawn, red as blood, pure as fire, sharp as steel, cold as truth, until the sun warms us in the full day of our triumph..."

I was running towards the crowd, the lesser risk now.

"...invincible. Let them turn loose the dogs of fascism. For every one of us they strike down, his blood will nourish a thousand..."

Bastards.

"...sowing dragon's teeth..."

I shook the big iron-barred gate into the square. The bastards had locked it. The ones who were running me down, or the police to contain the crowd.

"...shall destroy, the future rising in glory from our struggle..."

His voice was triumphant, the crowd answering.

The Yamaha had stopped, engine idling, backfire echoing between rain-streaked buildings.

"Now is the moment..."

The man from the bread van reached into the basket among the *baguettes* and *ficelles*.

"...seize our destiny..."

It glinted.

"You're late."

"I'm sorry."

"There's no point in going now."

"I'm sorry."

I should apologize for being alive.

All right, Dolbiac was angry, but he should be able to see from my face.

"If you're not there from the beginning..."

"I know."

The Plough Must Hurt the Earth. It was Hungarian and significant. One hundred and forty-five minutes of significance, no interval. It had been very well reviewed. Miss the opening and you missed the significance. "It makes the real world seem trivial"—*Les Temps modernes.* One of those.

Dolbiac was walking.

"Where are we going?"

"I'm going to have a drink."

The "I" registered. But he had waited in the rain, so I followed.

It was getting better. My pulse rate was dropping back through ninety, pupils contracting, adrenalin draining, hyperventilating still, oxygen deficit in the bloodstream, muscles burned it up. Reaction would come soon. But I was alive.

It wasn't skill or training. It had been luck in rue de l'Hirondelle and I knew it and that was why there'd be reaction.

The man had straightened up, knocking two loaves on the wet tarmac. He swivelled round holding the rifle, presumably automatic fire, distance seventy metres. I couldn't tell the make; what did it matter. American, Belgian, Russian, they wash around the world, legal, illegal, forged end-user certificates. Knowing the make doesn't help, not in a dead-end street.

I wasn't hearing the crowd in the square beyond the barred gate, or the blood in my ears. I was hearing the shot from the rifle, the one you never hear because the bullet travels faster than sound.

"I said, what do you want?"

He looked at me. "A glass of Alsace. No, get me a whisky."

He looked at me down the length of the barrel. There was no hiding place, no parked car for shelter. The single light clamped to the wall of a building had a halo of thin rain and cast grey light across me. There was a cheap hotel of sorts, shuttered, door barred against trouble spilling over from the rally; and two more buildings, dark and closed.

It had to be now. I made it across the road in a forward roll and he still hadn't fired. Then I saw why. He had no silencer. There was the growl of the crowd and the backfire of the Yamaha but the sound of a gunshot echoing between narrow buildings wouldn't be smothered. I was an uncertain target and he needed first time success. It was his profession not an evening's sport.

"Are you all right?"

The glass in my hand was empty.

"Co? Co?"

The tone was abrupt but something of his anger was draining

I looked in Dolbiac's face. Some men are beautiful, like Nureyev or Valentino. Others create a different effect, like Bogart or Belmondo. Dolbiac was no pretty boy; there was strength in his face, directness in his eyes, confidence in his body.

"They killed Agate today." It came out. I couldn't keep all of it inside. I didn't want to talk about what had nearly happened to me, but the nerves needed release and I had to come out with something.

"Who's Agate? Do I know him?"

"No."

"What's he to do with you?"

The fist was iron and heavy. It was on grey painted doors, tall and double as if the building had stabled carriages in the top-hat days. A sign read: *Le Caveau de la Bolée. Club folklorique*. It was early evening, there must be a waiter preparing, a cleaner, a singer, someone.

He might as well have risked it. The iron knocker was like three gunshots.

"He tried to speak to me. A car hit him as he crossed the road."

"Who's they?"

"They?"

"You said they killed him."

"I don't know who they are." My voice was simple and slow, the body running down from its high. "I don't know."

The men on the Yamaha didn't like the seconds trickling away. Fifteen seconds, twenty seconds, and I was still alive. One was shouting to the man with the rifle, distracting him. I gained another four seconds of heartbeats.

"Well, who is he?"

Questions. As if I knew the answers. Dolbiac's eyes never wavered, like the first time I'd become aware of his intense gaze across the *terrasse* of the Café Soufflot.

"What did he want?" Dolbiac wouldn't let go, a possessive lover wanting every moment accounted for.

"Agate? I don't know. I'd never heard of him until..."

"Co, what the hell are you talking about?"

"Get me another drink."

"Are you drunk?"

They came out of the double doors in a torrent of repressed violence, iron purpose on their faces, muscles knotting in their

28

necks, abrupt taut movements. Had I given the signal, opened the floodgates?

"Get me another drink."

"For God's sake, I just did."

Drops of amber formed by the fumes slipped back down the inner slope of the glass. I drained the last of it.

Two dozen police with batons and riot-guards over the eyes and nose went pushing towards the rally, frustrated by the locked gates, came back, cursing, and I pressed against the wall.

Two cops shouted at me, rapid elided Parisian accents, something about knocking three blows, and I shook my head, waving down to the end of rue de l'Hirondelle.

The Yamaha and the bread van had gone.

"Can we go? Can I spend the night at your place?"

There was a middle-aged man at the next table in the bar, with the precise gestures of a small shopkeeper, perhaps a cheap jeweller. His wife was with him, something from the shop glittering at her throat. They stared.

"Why you?" Dolbiac asked. "People can't get killed just for speaking to you. How about me then?"

"I won't feel safe in my apartment."

"And me? Will I be safe?"

The middle-aged couple exchanged glances.

I walked to the end of the street and there was no one in sight, no bread van, no Yamaha. My foot crunched a loaf of bread.

"Co, what are you doing?"

The glass was in pieces on the floor, the sharp noise of it under foot, and the woman had that French face of shocked middle-aged disapproval, head tipped back, face long, mouth open, lower lip indrawn, hand clutching at the bauble at her throat. The husband was dabbing at her skirt with a handkerchief and saying something. I don't know what.

"Jesus, you're stoned." Dolbiac put a hand on my shoulder.

Then I began to shake.

I'm not aware of the moon in Paris. Man has killed it with headlights and street lamps and neon.

Tonight it suddenly broke through heavy clouds and I noticed its dead light, coming through the window, across his shoulders. There was something of the wild in Dolbiac, not just physically in the hairs on his chest and his strength. There was a fierceness in his love-making, as if it were vital to him to have possession of his mate. I'd loved him for that and for the contradictions, his intenseness, his creative vision. It was like having two lovers, a harmless form of bigamy.

It wasn't finished yet. The last ripples of shock still disturbed my brain and wouldn't surrender to sleep.

Dolbiac faced the wall, his breathing regular and slow. He had a hand resting on the duvet. The fingers were long and slender, and stretched wider than an octave and a half. Pianist's hands, lover's hands.

The clock in the church struck half past what. I would know when it struck the hour. It did it twice in case you misheard the first time.

Perhaps I should take one of the pills in the bathroom. I wouldn't be rested in the morning.

Not chloral hydrate. That had been for the big sleep.

I thought suddenly of Crevecoeur. Breakheart. He must have done that often enough.

"*Arc de Triomphe.*"

"Horse race."

"*Quatorze juillet.*"

"*La Bastille.*"

"*Ladouceur.*"

"Softness."

"Orange."

"Holland."

But his face was already changing, like watching the life go out of someone, the same features but more distant and without meaning. Somewhere in there was the reason for his visit, the connection with Agate, why I had been at the wrong end of the rifle. It made no sense to me. Nor was it meant to.

The sound of a car backfiring shattered the fragile peace and woke the ghosts in my head.

"Canuck."

I spoke the name softly and Dolbiac didn't respond. When we were alone I called him that.

I laid a hand on his hip and slipped it over to rest between his thighs. I heard the rhythm of his breathing change.

"Canuck, my brain's got on a rollercoaster, up and down and back again, and it won't stop."

After the pause his breathing had gone on, slow and deep, but now it was because he made the conscious effort. I waited because he wanted me to. A petty form of punishment and I thought: It's not the first time in recent weeks.

"Canuck, you're not still angry about the Kisfaluddy play?"

He turned over.

"If they killed him this morning, why were you late this evening?"

He'd had time to think too.

"I got caught up in the rally in place St-Michel."

"St-Michel? Why were you there?"

"I had the idea someone was following me."

"Because of this morning? What was this guy to you?"

"Please."

I couldn't tell. We could eat together and go to plays together and make love together, but the wall was round the core of my life and I could let no one climb in. I was alone there.

"Was he..."

"Canuck."

I stopped his questions.

The body was released. The brain still wouldn't let go.

I had been trained to think. I isolated four conclusions and only the last gave the slightest comfort.

Agate had tried to communicate something in which the Agency was involved, the exposure of which would damage its credibility, reputation or aims; Crevecoeur was concerned that I had found this out, so his relationship with the Agency was a query; some group, unidentified, had tried to draw a thick red line through my name; but they had been concerned to lose my death in the confusion of the election rally, so they felt the need for some care.

I had become involved because of my past.

I was trained, body and mind, skills and knowledge, by the Agency. In that respect Agate and I were at one. I had reached a similar conclusion to Agate, but at a much earlier stage. The Agency is a vast bureaucracy and a bureaucracy should not decide questions of life and death. It functions in the way of all man-made machines, never questioning its aims, condoning and concealing errors, concerned at its own survival, with a career-structure and people ambitious for promotion. There are vertical lines of command but where are the horizontal lines tying down the whole machine? It got out of control under Kennedy and no one has been strong enough to impose his authority.

I can't accept corporate decisions because they deny you are an individual. I make my own decisions, how I should act, about right and wrong. I cannot accept that a subcommittee sitting in an air-conditioned office on the other side of the world should decide what I do. I will not be Item 7(c) on an agenda.

In the end there were a dozen reasons, big and small, why I could no longer be part of it but it was "bed and board" that was the final trigger. "Cody, if we tell you to shack up with Comrade X because we think it's necessary, you'll do it." The Agency doesn't officially use the term "bed and board"; it uses the practice.

It is me, my life, my body. I make the decisions.

I had learned a lot in four years' training. They were not happy when I left.

When my life in Washington with Martin fragmented into a million pieces, I ran to Dulles airport, wanting to put distance between us. It was Madrid first, then Paris. For some Americans Europe is a continual irritant, a stubborn insistence on being different. For others it is a release. I was at ease.

My training wasn't wasted, because there are always people willing to pay for certain skills. But I don't ever wake in the night and cry out: "I'm sorry, I didn't want to, it was the subcommittee in Langley ordered me."

We thought the trials at Nuremberg had disposed of that defence. It lives.

4

He stood naked in the centre of the room.

I watched, not for erotic reasons.

I watched because it was a relationship going sour and his actions might hold a clue to his reasons. We always look for the cause in others not ourselves.

His long fingers stretched, arched through the air, met his toes, hands to his side, upstretch, recommence. There are artists who protest the body is unimportant, a house for the mind. Dolbiac was different.

He brought coffee. I held out a hand and he sat on the edge of the bed.

He said: "I have to be at rue de Madrid this evening." It was vague. I didn't press him.

32

By eight o'clock he was in his living room/studio, at the piano set against the wall, with no window on a distracting world. He worked for two hours with total concentration. He emptied his mind for ten minutes. He worked for another two hours. Then he stopped. Most afternoons he went to the Conservatoire: their youngest professor of piano composition, signal honour for a foreigner, a French-Canadian. My Canuck.

"I compose every morning," Schubert explained. "As soon as one piece is finished I begin another."

Dolbiac followed Schubert's example, not his music. Perhaps he would be a Boulez, more likely a Berio or a loner like Panufnik. I couldn't understand his music or the mind that produced it. My stubbornness irritated him.

"Composing music is a creative act. How do you expect to explain any act of creation?"

"But I can look at a painting or a sculpture. I hear the conversations that go into a novel. There are connections with the real world. I don't see any lumps of music lying out there as inspiration."

We'd been in bed at the time. Funny pillow talk.

"The inspiration is interior. You can learn rhythm, stress, harmonics, natural affinities of chords. You can be taught theory; like the chord progression of Dominant to Tonic is nearly always used at the end because it sounds like finishing off. But the melodic line, the innovation, the total conception come from within. In your head, Co, it is silent. In my head, when I exclude everything else, there is music."

I left him at the piano. He wasn't aware of my going. For me there was the problem of my apartment, problem for me alone.

They knew where I lived because the tail had picked me up on the corner. The apartment was no longer secure, but it had things I needed. They might come knocking at any time, and when I opened the door there would be the blue-black nose with one nostril and the quiet farewell.

I would never be safe because they thought I knew a secret, that Agate had spoken.

I was ignorant.

I sat at a table by the plate-glass window of the Café Charlot, fingers laced round a brown cup, eyes on the outside world. The rain had gone, the sky was clear; a bitter north-easterly blowing the clouds away. There were people passing with coat collars turned up, stopping, shaking hands, hiding their hands again in

33

pockets. They talked of the weather; you could tell from their glances at the sky. It felt more like February than November. Some of the faces I recognized; the woman from the dry-cleaners, one of the young men from the back room of the butchery, the man who spent his nights wrapped in newspaper on the métro grating on boulevard St-Germain and his days plucking at sleeves. He got little from housewives, careful with their shopping money, had more luck with students.

Ten minutes.

The green van came past for the second time. No name on the side and the anonymity snagged my attention. It found a gap between the parked cars and stopped. Two minutes. Three minutes. Nobody got out.

I paid for the coffee and left, turning away from the little van. Four right turns brought me round the block, the van facing me, fifty metres distance. I was in the cover of a tall revolving metal pyramid of paperbacks outside the magazine store. I picked a Simenon, letting myself become part of the street furniture.

I read at random.

"Elle essaya de lui sourire..."

The garish cover altered the image of my face.

"On la sentait nerveuse..."

I was moving gradually out from cover.

"Elle continuait à observer la rue comme si elle eût craint de voir surgir quelqu'un..."

Yes. My eyes edged over the book.

The driver of the van sat, eyes down, speaking to someone unseen, lips moving in a monologue.

There was nobody in the seat beside him.

My eyes tracked along the street. Checked other vehicles. Checked doorways. Checked windows. Checked rooftops. There was only one flat roof but there were chimneys on other roofs, natural cover for a man with an X4 telescopic sight and a radio warning of a target. The skyline seemed clean.

The business of the street was normal. In the block behind was an area of shops and street market, stalls of clementines and bananas and Beurre Hardy pears, crabs and shrimps, sausages from Auvergne and Provence. There could be a man lost in that crowd, receiver like a deaf aid plugged in his ear, automatic in the holster under his arm.

But they wouldn't want so many witnesses: they had tried to disguise my death the night before.

I convinced myself.

I replaced the book and walked down the street, directly at the van, passing close to its window.

Some feel disappointment, some even feel anger, but if they do they are in the wrong business and unlikely to survive in it long. The time isn't wasted, never wasted, taking precautions. It could be twenty minutes spent and I'd drawn blank. The next time it saves your life, and who can argue against that? There's a word for those who do: "dead".

The driver had *L'Equipe* on his knees, lips moving, stumbling over the three-syllable words. I passed and checked in his door mirror but he had no interest in me. I was in the clear. I could go in.

"*Mlle Cody.*"

"*Oui, Mme Boyer.*"

Every building in Paris has one, waiting in a glass-fronted spyhole on the world. If they don't spy for the police, they do it for fun. She was an ample woman, in black since her husband had been killed in the war. The Germans hadn't got him. He'd drunk too much Calvados and fallen under a truck of de Gaulle's Free French. She had voted for de Gaulle faithfully until he died.

"They came about your carpet."

Yes. That was more the style than a little green van in a crowded street.

"When?"

"Quite early this morning. You were not in. I told them you had not been in all night and I couldn't say when you'd be back."

She had the nose for looking down but not the height.

"What did they say they wanted with the carpet?"

"To clean it, of course. It's your carpet. You should know."

"Of course, I forgot."

Other childless women of her age keep a poodle. Mme Boyer could show affection only to a geranium in a pot. She held an arm in front of its pink flowers as if to protect it from me.

I turned to go up.

"They made a lot of noise, and in the end didn't take the carpet. They said they'd have to come back."

I froze, one foot on the stairs, the other in the grave.

"You let them in my apartment? When I wasn't there?"

"What am I supposed to do, when you have the habit of spending the night elsewhere?"

35

"Did you stay with them?"

"I am too busy. There was the hall to sweep and everything."

I began to climb and the concierge followed half a dozen steps behind, aggrieved.

"It was most inconvenient of you giving me no instructions. Young people today have no consideration, they are always so concerned with their own affairs, and Monsieur Roussy was truly upset about the noise they made, hammering and knocking..."

"Mme Boyer, don't let anyone in my apartment. Nobody."

"Nobody? Monsieur Dolbiac?"

"They could be burglars."

"Burglars? They showed me your name on their call sheet. It was typed."

"Burglars can type."

"If you have any complaints, the police should go in first."

"No police." No doubt Crevecoeur would hear anyway.

I stopped in front of the door to my apartment, Mme Boyer watching. If they wanted to kill me—and they did—it could be the door handle, or the keyhole, or pushing the door open. Beyond the door was the jungle.

"Alors..." She used her sniff.

Key turning in the lock, handle depressed, door swinging open and the only noise came from the hinge that needed oil.

We looked. There was no chaos. Mme Boyer took a breath to continue and I went inside one step and shut the door.

I kept absolutely still. And then the senses sharp one by one: hearing, smell, sight.

There was no answering stimulus, but the apartment held the bruised air of intruders.

In Berlin I had watched a bulldozer turn up an unexploded wartime bomb. The workmen went to earth like rabbits. I was behind a wall with two of them and after some moments they began to look at one another, trying to read the future in each other's eyes, not speaking because of the uncertainty. Was there a fuse burning? Was the timing mechanism ticking again? I had ducked for cover like them but I didn't feel with their nerves. Now I did: because I had to go in.

What should I look for? I couldn't get inside their minds and didn't know where to start.

Five steps along the wall and I was at the entrance to the living room. Start here.

First the carpet because there could be a pressure pad, and

until I established that was secure I was boxed in.

They said they'd come about the carpet, the hammering being part of their cover. I worked all over it. The carpet was safe.

There was no plastic explosive on light bulbs waiting for warmth to detonate it. I checked plugs, sockets and wiring for short circuits.

Chairs, cushions, under the feet of the desk.

I began on the track for the curtain across the window and then I felt damp spring in the palms of my hands. I'd been so concerned with this room I'd ignored other rooms.

How many windows across the road overlooked me? I should have checked that first and my pulse was running away at the memory of the rifle glinting among the loaves of bread.

I used a handmirror round the frame, checking each window opposite in turn. There was the problem of penetrating the dark interiors of the rooms because my pupils were adjusting for the sunlit exterior of the buildings. It took patience but if there were a rifle, no matter if the man stood back, there would be the eventual gleam of reflected light.

There was only the old man staring at the goldfinch in its cage.

I moved to the bedroom. Probing the bed took time. Mattress, pillows, duvet. No poison needle, no seam slit to insert a plastic deflator bag.

Kitchen.

The cold water came direct from the mains, should be safe. But there was the cistern that supplied hot water to the sink and the bathroom. It was conceivable they'd introduced something into the tank. Hydrocyanic acid, for instance. I'd run a hot bath, step in, breathe the vapour. The bath would grow cold, so would my body. I moved the mixer arm over the waste outlet and ran the hot until the water from the tank came cold.

Food was the easiest of all to tamper with, the hardest to check. Throw it all away? Eggs, butter, salami, olive oil...

The telephone rang in the living room.

And I stopped, hand touching the receiver, mind focusing on it; black plastic instrument, repeated ringing. Everybody is conditioned to pick up the phone without thought, absolute reflex action, and I hadn't checked it.

It was ringing, insistent on being answered, and what happened when the receiver was lifted?

Still ringing, and I took the umbrella from the hall, crouched behind the desk, knocked the instrument to the floor. False worry.

No, no worry was false because they'd tried to get me once and they'd penetrated the apartment once while I was out.

The phone no longer rang except in my head, like an alarm unheeded on a building all night.

"Hello?"

Nothing.

I replaced the phone on the desk and at once it rang again.

"Yes."

"Cody?"

"Who is it?"

"Are you Cody? I can't take any risk."

"What do you mean?"

"Confirm."

"It's Cody. Who are you?" I didn't recognize the voice, accent a little on the Bogart side, funny way with the "r" when he said "risk".

"It's a business without names, you know that."

"What do you want?"

"They got Agate but that's not the end of it. I know what he wanted to communicate."

"Tell me."

"Not the phone. It could have ears."

"Go on."

"In person and it's got to be at once because there's no time."

"Where?"

"You know the Vert Galant on the Île de la Cité?"

"Yes."

"The very tip of the garden. No one can overhear."

"All right. How do I..."

"I know what you look like. I'll have my Polaroid camera. I'll ask you to take my picture."

"What..."

"No questions, there's no time. Leave now."

Gone. I stared at the receiver. Just a steady tone.

Then I saw it, red and yellow plastic behind the seven holes. I unscrewed the earpiece and the transmitter rested in the palm of my hand, size of a sugar cube. Smash it? Then they'd know I'd discovered it and pay another visit. Shut it in a closet and let it transmit harmlessly?

And then I dropped the bug and was running for the door, running because of what they'd overheard. How long would it take them to reach the Vert Galant, to reach my source of information and put a hand over his mouth?

I took the stairs two at a time, and then into the street, a Pekinese snapping, darting in front of a 2CV with a horn, like a sheep in the rain, the length of rue Dauphine, with my mind on nothing but running because I had to get there before them, slipping between women with fat hips and men who turned to stare, and at the end there were red traffic lights on the Quai.

They'd got everything else just right.

Long seconds.

There was no possibility of dodging between the Renaults and Simcas. The traffic cop glared, white gloves fluttering, whistle between his teeth; glared and released his tension bawling at cretins, ridiculing driver or pedestrian. I couldn't risk going against the lights because he'd vent his frustration on me for half a minute.

Thirty seconds could be the margin.

They'd got everything else just right but they hadn't allowed for the red light.

I waited, toes gripping the kerbstone.

They hadn't calculated that the brain, racing because of the phone call and the Agate information and the bug in the receiver, would spin down a new track as I was held back.

Delay builds panic or lets it subside. Everything had been arranged to encourage panic to flood the nerves, no possibility of slowing and letting the brain function. Now I began to think.

When the light turned green and the whistle blew, I had drawn breath, and suspicion had lodged in my mind.

They had shown themselves deliberately when they came to my apartment, and why? Why risk the bug being found? Because it was done to create panic.

Time was 10.43 and it had taken me six minutes. I kept on the east side of Pont Neuf, going fast but alert to possibilities now, skirting the Place, crossing to the far side of the Seine, then returning over the bridge.

There was Henry IV on a horse and the steps and the Square du Vert Galant, no square by a triangle.

Lovers, children and fishermen have time to stop and dream beside water. There was the unceasing roar of traffic and the treble cries of small boys with a ball.

The lamp on the bridge was small protection, the real protection being that I wasn't approaching from the expected direction.

An artist had his easel set up to face the stone bridge and the Monnaie on the left bank, his back to me. From my position the

39

angle of the canvas was too oblique too see. He seemed to be applying blue sky; obsessed with blue sky.

A man in a frayed coat squatted on the ground, drinking from a bottle, fishing rod taking care of itself.

The tourists came streaming across the road, I didn't see where they sprang from; all men in their twenties and thirties, jeans and sweaters and windcheaters. Some had cameras and as they strung out going down the steps I checked Leica, Nikon, Rollei. No Polaroid.

I noticed the wind. I'd had no time to reach for a coat.

Polaroid man came alone. He stopped by the steps, camera to his eye, looking across the bridge to the left bank as if trying to frame a shot. Then he scrutinized the gravel and grass of the little garden.

He wore a padded denim jacket, had black hair and a short black beard.

I could have shouted.

The tourists had lined up, the Louvre a distant grey backdrop, while a man looked through the viewfinder of his Leica.

Polaroid man started down the steps and I could have shouted. I ducked below the wall until he turned away from my position on the bridge. He walked towards the tip, where the island juts into the Seine like the prow of a boat.

A tourist in a Southern Comfort sweatshirt looked round to check the sun and waved a hand and photographed the group.

There was a speedboat, whispering its power, idling up against the current. It had a pocket-size pennant that snapped in the wind. The man at the throttle wore a peaked cap and a roll-neck sweater. His two companions wore photochromatic glasses.

Polaroid man skirted the willow tree at the tip of the garden. Its branches were bare but he peered behind the trunk, checked all round.

I could have waved.

He put a cigarette in his mouth, came back to the artist, got a light, said something and it could have been thank you.

He moved back to the willow tree, ducking under a branch. He drew on the cigarette, tiny cloud of grey snatched away by the wind.

The artist picked up his easel and moved ten metres nearer the tree.

Nearly eight minutes the group had spent snapping souvenir shots.

40

Superficially it was so right. They had wound up the tension, an hour and a half on my own searching the apartment for death, then pulled the trigger with the anonymous call and the bug in the telephone. The urgency should have shot me straight down among a dozen of them. There was even the boat in case I dived.

Overkill.

"Mme Boyer, have there been any callers?"

"No, Mlle Cody, there have been none."

Eyes followed me up the stairs.

Driving licence, passport, money from the spine of *Larousse Gastronomique* in the kitchen. No more. Nothing to make it look as if I were running. No suitcase when I passed Mme Boyer again.

It took two minutes. In another five minutes, ten minutes, they'd conclude I wasn't coming to the Vert Galant and they'd return.

They'd missed twice. The third time they'd make certain, even if it were crude.

I took a taxi along boulevard St-Germain, paid it off at the lights of rue St-Jacques, caught one going the other way, paid it off at rue Vaugirard, ducked into the Luxembourg Gardens. There were boys playing at sailors with yachts on the pond; Don't walk on the grass; even the gravel looked disciplined.

I was satisfied. I'd brought no one.

5

And then I found what I had been hooked into.

The man asked my name and I said it was Black and he wrote *Blaque* in a lined school exercise-book with a faded blue cover and said it was fifty-eight francs a night, in advance. I had no luggage.

The Hotel Moderne was a lie.

I sat in a room where the floorboards had worn a ridge through the maroon patterned carpet. There was a basin and a bidet in the corner, a modesty screen streaked with soapy splashes, a notice pinned by the mirror forbidding the washing of clothes. The bed sagged in the centre where bodies had closed together.

41

There was grey net over the lower half of the window, a view of a tenement buttressed with thick timber, shouts of children from a school out of sight, drifting smells of frying garlic and ginger from a Chinese restaurant.

"...if I didn't like it, that was too damn bad. The scenario was final, there'd be no rewrites..."

Agate's words. The secret had been locked in his brain and hadn't been able to find the key.

Crevecoeur's catalogue of phrases held a clue, but I needed a clue to find the clue.

They'd driven me towards the election rally in place St-Michel and was that significant? Or the opposite: my theory was mistaken, they hadn't driven me, they were following and were concerned that I shouldn't see the rally.

It is no good rejecting the unlikely when you are ignorant. There were a thousand improbabilities. Test and eliminate, test until you hit the right button. I needed some point of departure.

I started with the *Herald-Trib*, but that concerned itself with bigger things. SALT 3, Soviet dissidents, Mondale's Latin American jaunt, Giscard's election speech in Lyon, coffee futures firmer, three killed in Soweto township riots. The rally in place St-Michel was nowhere. No clue.

Le Figaro gave it half a column, not a big splash. *Le Courrier* gave it more prominence, but even there it was below the fold, only eight injured, nobody killed, story continued on page sixteen; and when I turned to the continuation it hit me right below the heart. There, next to the follow-up. I studied three short paras and a smudgy head-and-shoulders shot out of the archives.

Mystery of missing scientist.

Jean-Louis Ladouceur, Head of Environmental Studies at the Institut 21, has been missing from his post since last Friday. Ladouceur, 32, one of the most brilliant young scientists at the Think Tank, blah blah.

There was more, but it didn't help.

By leaning my head against the wall and peering up I could see a corner of the sky. The artist in the garden of the Vert Galant, blobbing the stuff on with a palette knife, hadn't been exaggerating. It was an icy blue, a sky swept clean by a wind that felt as if it had blown from Siberia.

"*Quatorze juillet.*"

"*La Bastille.*"

"*Ladouceur.*"

"Missing scientist."

I knew the correct catechism now. I appreciated Crevecoeur, leading up to it part in English, part in French, so that *Ladouceur* hadn't seemed an obvious probe point.

Just knowing about Ladouceur would be enough to kill me?

"Pasquier, I think. I'm almost certain. He uses American phrases like 'think tank' and 'megadeath' and 'wheeler-dealer'."

He was a plump man; thinning hair that dropped dandruff on his shoulders, Gauloise in the corner of his mouth drifting smoke in one eye and ash on his lapel. Like all journalists who need both hands to take notes and type, he'd grown used to talking without removing the cigarette from his lips. He used two fingers on the typewriter in a burst of energy, muttered *"Merde"* and backtracked to xxx out an error.

There was the mixture of sounds that make up the newsroom in a newspaper building: typewriter keys, flimsy being wrenched out of the roller, telephones insistent, shouts and murmurs. Somebody had brought in a bottle of Johnnie Walker and men were dumping coffee dregs in the wpb to get a shot.

"That's his desk."

It had a jumble of papers, an old Adler typewriter, a drawer that wouldn't close. Beside the desk a secretary was banging at a filing cabinet with a drawer that wouldn't open. On the wall was a tear-sheet from *Twen* of Maria Schneider. It was a tableau that summed up life in the *Courrier* office.

"Where do I find Pasquier?" I asked.

The man shrugged. He peered at a notebook. If it had been shorthand, he would have found it easier. The notes were scribbled abbreviations, initial letters followed by a scrawl. Marchais would complain of misquotation again.

"Is he at home?"

"Home?" The reporter glanced at me briefly.

"Is he out on a job?"

"Hey Jo-Jo," the reporter shouted. "Is Pasquier working?"

"I've never noticed it."

A boy came past whistling, lifting a plastic cup of black coffee from a filing tray, spilling a little on the reporter's notebook.

"*Ah, la vache.*"

The man dabbed with a tissue at the darkening patch.

"Has he got a bar he goes to? How about dinner?"

"The Café Dupont over the road, Bar La Jument, Chez Jean. Sometimes he eats at Les Trois Marias."

The editorial offices of *Le Courrier* had been seedy like a secondhand-furniture warehouse and the bars had a similar air of despair and gullibility. No Pasquier.

In Les Trois Marias the waiter paused with a tray of dishes to nod at a man at a table in the back.

Pasquier was facing the room, must have observed the waiter's gesture, paid no attention as I moved between tables.

His hair was chestnut and elegantly disarranged in a *coupe sauvage,* features finely chiselled, hands moving like a hare dodging away across a field.

"You're Pasquier?"

He looked at me, blinked, nodded.

"I'm Cody."

"Yes." He said nothing else as I sat down, totally uncurious.

"You wrote a piece about Ladouceur, the missing scientist."

"Well?"

"What's so important about Ladouceur?"

Pasquier was eating *poulet basquais,* blood-red sauce running into fluffy rice. He picked up the wing, tearing off the flesh with little white teeth. Twice his eyes went up to my face. I waited.

"Cody," he said, and I knew my name was filed away in his memory: the woman who was asking for Ladouceur. "And what's so important about Ladouceur for you?"

"Was Ladouceur a friend of Agate?" I asked.

"Now who is Agate?"

"You don't know him?"

"I don't recognize the name."

"American, early thirties, about 1 metre 80, 75 kilos, light wavy hair, pale face, long nose." I left out the bit about the four days' stubble, and the core office and being murdered.

"Could be a thousand people. Nothing special?"

"Agate wanted to tell me something about Ladouceur, but he didn't. So I want to find Ladouceur, ask him myself."

"A lot of people want to find him."

"Why is he so important?" Full circle, but he mightn't notice now he'd started to talk.

"Because of the Institut 21."

"What does that do?"

He dropped the naked bone on his plate, transferred his whole attention to me.

"Amazing. They accuse the press of vulgarizing and trivializing because we make things understandable. We succeed because we're popular because we're interesting because we simplify. But you've never heard of Institut 21; therefore we've failed."

He returned to his plate, digging his fork into tomato and red pepper and explosive *loukenka* sausage.

"You wrote it was a think tank."

"Right. The bureaucrats wanted to give it some drab name like the Institute for the Study of Options in the Twenty-first Century, copied off the cover of the file in the Ministry. The press called it Institut 21, and the name stuck."

He dipped a piece of crust into the sweet-sharp sauce.

"It's a government agency?"

"Ah." He considered his plate, and pushed it away. "It's very French in its structure, big business and government in bed together and you don't know who's doing what to whom. Some of the Dassault millions may have found their way there, not unconnected with resolving the tax scandal is the whisper; and there's oil money from the Arabs, denied but true; and it's organized by bright boys from the Ministry of Finance all tutoying each other. Giscard is mad keen on it, just his style, intellectual, advanced technology, surface glitter."

The waiter came up and said there was a telephone call. When Pasquier had left, he picked up the used plate and turned to me.

"*Vous désirez quelque chose, mademoiselle?*"

"*Merci.*"

My eyes were on Pasquier's back as he leaned on the bar, speaking with his right hand cupping the mouthpiece, occasional darting movement of his free hand. I didn't want to lose him, lose momentum.

"*Le plat du jour, c'est...*"

"*Pas faim.*"

Pasquier came back, afterglow of a smile on his face. I had the feeling, we all get it sometimes, that I had been talked about.

"What do they do at the Institut?"

"They invent the future."

He must have used the cliché often in his paper.

"And does it work?" I asked.

Pasquier poured half a glass of wine, taking his time.

Paris restaurants aren't what they were. They never have been, of course, except the Tour d'Argent, Lasserre, Maxim's, where only the prices change. Self-service and Vietnamese capture whole streets. There's a McDonald's on the Champs-Elysées pumping out Big Macs and French Fries. But Les Trois Marias made no concessions. The check tablecloths had paper on top which waiters used to write the bills; four men at the *zinc* stood each other Pernods; the napkins of regulars were pigeonholed into a wooden rack; a fat woman in black at the cash register counted each slice of *tarte maison;* there was *tête de veau vinaigrette* in mauve ink on the menu; and sounds of efficient hysteria from the kitchen.

"Yes, they think it works." Pasquier said. "It comes with a thirty-five minute guarantee."

I waited. "All right, I buy. What is the thirty-five minute guarantee?"

"Cruise time from the missile silos near Lvov."

The waiter brought over a round marble slab.

"What specifically do they do at the Institut 21?"

Pasquier opened a box with a picture of Napoleon on the front. He sniffed and nodded to the waiter.

"Have some cheese."

"Not now."

"The camembert is in perfect condition. It's difficult to get a good camembert now."

"What do they do?"

"They pasteurize the milk and the result is the cheese is never..."

"Not that."

He wasn't right. His behaviour didn't fit.

"Lot of glamour, lot of *razzmatazz.*" He could have been describing a Busby Berkeley set piece, his mobile hands giving extra force to the antique slang. "Giscard finds it fits his notion of France leading Europe into the next century. Interesting thing is that when you put a lot of thinkers together in a *multi-discipline hothouse,*" again the hands emphasizing the English phrase, "and fertilize them with millions of francs, something exotic usually grows."

He was full of information. Don't reporters ask questions?

"The disciplines are: the Mind, the Body, the Environment, the Social Structure; with a lot of the studies cutting across boundaries."

"Do they publish reports?"

"When it suits them. Surely you heard of the Algerian project this summer?"

"No."

Pasquier poured from the bottle again and swirled his glass. "Wine," he announced, holding up the glass, fingers delicately extended, in a piece of pure theatre. Only a Frenchman could do it and not look as if he were acting.

"The Algerian government was concerned because the world doesn't value their wine. It is too coarse, too heavy, too full of tomorrow's hangover. They approached the Institut 21 for help and Ladouceur asked to work on it. You must understand that Ladouceur strongly approves of Algeria because it is revolutionary."

"He's a marxist?"

"Let me put it this way: if he met Karl and Groucho at a *cocktail,* he would talk to Karl." He smiled to himself. "Ladouceur was absolutely brilliant. He had sample bottles sent from all the winegrowing areas along the Algerian coastal strip. He dehydrated each bottle and analysed the congenerics—that is what is left after the alcohol and water have evaporated, what gives each wine its unique flavour. Just from analyzing the mineral salts that had passed from the soil to the grapes to the wine he drew up a report for the Algerian government: you've got iron deposits under this vineyard, coal under there, manganese, copper, so forth. No expensive geological surveys, no time wasted. A dozen bottles of wine, one week in the laboratory, one man, one computer. Brilliant."

Agate had been killed trying to pass some information about Ladouceur to me. Not this. Not some Jesus-miracle turning wine into iron and coal and copper.

"Have you seen the Institut?"

"No," I said.

"Right out of science fiction." He seemed to consider describing it and shook his head. "They play with ideas and let the computer do the work. And the computer, it's..." He paused again, groping for the right words. "Well, it's very big, very expensive, very twenty-first century, and the government was unhappy about having an American machine in there. Especially since it needs a dozen crewcuts from IBM writing the programs and nursing it when it gets indigestion."

"They're unhappy about Americans being there?"

"Yes."

"Why?"

"Why do you think?"

I could think of reasons. I could think of a line of communication

that went from Agate through the computer programmers to
Ladouceur. It's not the sort of thought you volunteer. But Pasquier
did it for me.

"A little clue," he said. "The US Defence Department spent
over ten billion dollars with IBM in the sixties and early seventies
alone. *Money talks, okay?*" His accent wasn't specific, probably
picked up from Hollywood movies.

And why wasn't he asking questions? Who was I, where did I
live, what did I want to know for?

"Does Ladouceur have a current project?"

"Obviously, but nobody will say. Very hush, confidentiality of
clients, the usual excuses they bring out when they don't want
to be embarrassed."

"No pointers?"

"No. So we'll print rumours, see which they deny. When they
say there's absolutely no truth in the speculation that..." He
turned his hand palm up on the table. "His section dealt with
the environment, which is broad enough. But he took a special
interest in climatology and geo-economics. Big words. If it doesn't
rain in Normandy, where he has a non-marxist country house by
the way, if there's no rain, then no grass, no cows, no camembert.
That's how a journalist vulgarizes climatology and geo-economics."

"No note, no debts, no love affair?"

"Nothing we've found out yet." Pasquier had his left hand on
his leg, but I saw his glance go down to his watch. My time was
up. "Listen, give me your phone number. If I find out something
I can't put in the paper, I'll let you know."

"633.83.50."

He wrote it on a corner of the paper tablecloth, added "Cody",
tore it off and put it in his pocket.

6

First I met a streetwalker. Then I got a kerbcrawler.

But how?

If I understood how, I'd know who. It made a difference.

The tails I'd had the evening before had been running me down
into a death trap. They'd shown themselves at the turnings where

I had a choice of directions and it was like beaters heading a twelve-pointer away from the hills down the forest path straight into the cross-hairs of the .475. But these?

One in a Datsun Cherry, I couldn't see the face properly. One, that I could see, on foot.

How? I'd been clean before.

The one on foot I'd picked up crossing the place de la République after leaving Pasquier in Les Trois Marias. I'd turned to check traffic and in peripheral vision seen the man in the raincoat duck his head down into a paper. The abruptness registered. I crossed when the traffic let me and walking down the Avenue I stopped to sneeze, using a Kleenex from my shoulderbag, and as I put it back slipped out the vanity mirror, brief check, and he slowed and stopped, pretending to look for a break in the traffic.

They'd have called him "Ginger" at school. Maybe they still did, he was young enough. He had red hair, wispy red moustache, pale skin, upright way of carrying himself. His face was pinched from the evening air, the breath came in little puffs from his mouth as if he were smoking. It was cold. I thought there'd be a frost later on. I felt it at my heart already.

I connected with the Datsun at the traffic lights at the crossing with boulevard Richard Lenoir. He hesitated when the lights went green, cop waving, then crossed and stopped again. I turned right and the Datsun moved off. When I reached the next corner he'd circled the block, three consecutive right turns, and must have had luck with no one-ways.

The difference was whether they were after information or had close-the-file orders. Whoever they were.

How? It worried me. I'd been clean when I left the Hotel Moderne. Concierge at *Le Courrier?* I'd said I'd brought the article on the abortion scandal and the concierge had said the newsroom was on the second floor, staring with a look that implied the article was autobiography. No tail from him. It could be a chance encounter, but you always leave coincidence till last.

In basic training at the institute near Langley they'd gone through surveillance and counter-surveillance. How to recognize kerbcrawlers and streetwalkers and quick-change artists (check the feet: they'll dress the face and body differently, but overlook the shoes), what procedure to follow with solos, how to deal with teams. It'll be the same at the establishments in Sigulda and Surrey and Sulejowek. In the Psy B course, "Aunty" said: "I'll give you a simple way of telling whether you're being tailed for information or killing: let your tail know he's blown. If he wanted you to lead him somewhere or point out a contact, he'll give up when he knows he's blown because he recognizes it's a waste of time. Field Execs with trigger fingers will stay with you."

I turned right into Oberkampf. How do they choose their street names?

Datsun started.

I decided to throw them.

I went fifty metres to the corner with Voltaire, turned 180 degrees and walked straight back. Ginger was trying to dodge into a doorway. There were two women with a suitcase, a nun, a man exercising his dog; witnesses in case of rough stuff. Remember Agate. Remember the bread van. Remember the Vert Galant.

"How do I get to place de la République?"

He was no streetwalker. Streetwalkers, like the others of the name, are professional and don't blush. He muttered about turning right at the corner. I decided to rub his nose in it.

"That's where you started the tail, isn't it?"

He didn't like it.

I left him, turned right into Voltaire, checked. The Datsun had evaporated. I didn't see Ginger either and began to feel easier. I checked cars and pedestrians, always difficult at night in a restless city. The nun again. The nun, the nun. I overtook her, stopped abruptly.

"*Je vous demande pardon, ma soeur.*"

I put a hand out to steady her as I knocked her sideways. She was dumpy, sixty-five, shoes black and scuffed and low-heeled. Nuns have the most naked faces of all, concealing nothing. Not the nun.

I walked on. Place de la République.

Then they came again.

Ginger had retraced his route and was breathing heavily in a travel agent's doorway. The Datsun was tucked in the service entry to a café.

It was going to be the métro and it was going to be fast, which would shake the Datsun. I walked steadily, letting them observe from their semi-concealment, then abruptly into the métro entrance, the steps at the double, ticket ready in my hand, luck with a clear passage. I could hear the train in the tunnel, a sudden blockage of kids with backpacks, and Ginger made it after me, scrambling through, turning away, pretending.

How: it was urgent again. He hadn't been in any of the bars. He had striking hair I'd have noticed. The restaurant?

Ginger used a different door, same carriage. There was an evening crowd, not so jammed we couldn't watch each other.

The train jerked. Direction Châtelet. I wasn't taking him back to the Hotel Moderne.

How: was it Pasquier? Pasquier had seemed content when I left, only the woman in black at the cash desk had registered disapproval because I had spent nothing. And Pasquier only had one question, about my telephone number, and I'd given him the first figures that came into my head. Otherwise he'd been uninterested and that was uncharacteristic. I was a woman, asking questions about a missing scientist, and that to any journalist was a lead. It made sense now. He thought he'd learn more by following than by asking questions that got lies for answers.

Conclusion: they were amateurs. They were there for information but came back even when blown. "Aunty's" theory only worked when you played the professional game.

Ginger was standing, leaning against the door, masking his face with the paper. We all do it, but I wouldn't have chosen the *Courrier*.

The train left Hôtel de Ville and ran towards Châtelet. I didn't want him any further. I began to move.

I knew the how. Les Trois Marias, telephone call, Pasquier's cupped hand over the mouthpiece.

I pulled the newspaper down from his face.

"Did Pasquier tip you?"

He wasn't long out of college. He hadn't learned there are times you look a woman in the eyes and lie. His Adam's apple jiggled.

"Did he?" I crushed the paper with my knee.

His eyes widened and he nodded.

"Who was the kerbcrawler?"

"In the Datsun?"

"Yes."

"Durand."

"In case I took a taxi?"

"We thought you had a car."

His accent was clean and precise; home town somewhere in Berry among the flat hectares of boring wheat, come to Sin City to make his fame and fortune. He had just graduated from carrying the filing tray with cups of coffee. But check.

"What do you do?"

"On the sports page."

Right, the paper. But the sports page, as if tailing me were some kind of game.

"Follow the Tour de France, not me."

The train was slowing, lights ahead. I had my hand on the doorhandle.

"If you follow me, it'll be straight to a *flic*. I'll show him the bruise." I bunched the skin of my throat between thumb and forefinger and pressed. The weal would look red and angry for five minutes.

He was an amateur. The others weren't.

It's not the dark. It's the dark thoughts as you hear the clock strike two, three, four. Sometimes, when sleep comes, there are dreams. I have no defence.

When I woke I lay in the dark and the sweat was warm between my breasts. I wasn't sweating because of the temperature: I could feel the cold clutching at me through the window. It was the dream, and the other thing.

There was no one to talk to, to touch.

Canuck and I weren't together in the tunnel of that night, and as the echo of the dream subsided I suddenly knew: we wouldn't be together any longer. Perhaps once or twice more, a couple of tugs to wrench two lives apart. Nine months it had been.

At first it had been exhilaration and despair with Canuck, as it always is. The first time, before we went to bed, it had been like a hand clutching at the foot of my belly and I was breathing in shallow ripples. I felt a pain needing to be assuaged. As it always is. Then there was a lot of cat and dog; neither of us would bend. We progressed through a period almost of domesticity. But now I'd caught Dolbiac twice with that look on his face, tight male look of being aggrieved, little irritations getting big reactions, petty emotions flaring, and none of the sweet reconciliations of hot summer nights. And what does that mean but we'd lost it, he was getting itchy? Nothing more.

The dream was receding. There was still the other thing. It had been like this.

There'd been two more of them and I hadn't noticed them earlier because I had been preoccupied with the amateurs. These weren't amateurs.

They'd come up the métro steps ten seconds after me. I'd been checking Ginger didn't try to be naughty and they appeared together but separated without saying goodbye. I walked and when I rechecked they were both there, one each side of the road. They had hard cheeks and one chewed gum.

I was frightened.

I took them to rue de la Harpe, a jazz club in a cellar. The one who chewed gum sat on a stool, the other stood in shadow by the wall, glass of whisky breaking the line of his face. When the one on the stool reached for the bar telephone I knew I had to move: his jacket fell forward and I caught sight of the underarm holster. He spoke into the mouthpiece quietly, listened a little, his eyes checked once in my direction and he nodded. He must have grunted at the same time but we all use facial expressions and gestures on the telephone.

I chose a man on his own, a tourist from Milwaukee. I found that out when I said I'd have a beer and he warned me against it. We sat at a little table close to the jazz group and had to lean together to talk.

The group played 'Sleepy Time Down South', homage to Bechet who'd used the club.

The other two were waiting. There had been a wink between them.

I smiled a lot and played the little woman card quite shamelessly, because of the other two. I took the mirror out and put on a big expression of horror at how awful my face looked. Milwaukee man protested I looked great, but I had a hand on his shoulder, big promising smile down at him, and left for the little girl's room, as I called it. I didn't hurry. I even exaggerated the hip action of my walk.

I knew they'd be watching.

There was a short passage and at the end a disgusting kitchen. The Paris authorities had recently discovered fire, and an escape ladder led to a grating in the alley. I took the ladder, a little North African cook stirring at a pan of something and saying nothing.

When I was half-way up the rungs I heard voices and down below were my two tails moving across the kitchen. The one who chewed gum spat it out and felt under his arm. He was climbing the ladder, gun in hand, as I reached the top.

I thought I wasn't going to be able to do it. There was an agonizing moment as the ladder was vertical and then it was over and I heard his cry as he went over backwards. I think he missed the gas cooker.

I ran a block and stopped. I was alone.

By my shoulder there was a very old torn poster on the wall. This is what had got into my dream, not the man climbing the ladder or running through the shadows.

The poster had the bold heading *Le Chat d'Iran*. It showed this fat cat stalking among the mosques and oil wells, with workers like ants fleeing. The poster was in stark black and red, crude like a lino cut, and issued by the Students for a Democratic Iran. Red dripped from the cat's mouth. In my dream it was my body in the cat's mouth, the hot stink of its breath, its saliva dripping on my face, the ominous rumble of its purr. I was suffocating, teeth piercing my stomach and thighs and chest.

But I like cats.

It was the threatened violence of the last two days playing itself out in my unconscious, and I would feel more at ease in the morning. Small comfort in a lonely room.

Outside, Paris slept as much as Paris ever does. Burglars, police, *les filles* and insomniacs went about their night games. Inside, my brain picked and twisted and whichever way you looked at it, my life was untenable.

An American, some part of the Intelligence community, had started to run because he couldn't stomach something, and had been killed. Because I was the person he tried to reach, two attempts had been made on my life. A scientist working on a hush project was missing. A journalist tried to have me followed. The police had checked me out and now there was a green dossier with my name typed on the front joining four million others in the Sûreté Nationale.

My thoughts lay jumbled together. I must have slept again because I focused with a start on a patch of grey on the curtain and there was a thought in my mind that I had my passport and I should get out, take the plane to Stockholm or Casablanca, anywhere where they wouldn't be tracking me down.

It was a night thought. I wouldn't have had it if my brain was running smoothly because it was hopeless. I didn't know who they were. It could be the French and at the airport there'd be some query about the passport and would I mind stepping through this door. It could be the KGB and when I arrived in Stockholm or Casablanca I'd get in the wrong taxi, the one without handles inside the doors. It could be the Americans and where would I run from them?

I don't work for any organization, though how could I ever prove a negative? Once they learn you've been trained in Virginia, they believe you must be working under deep cover or have defected. You cannot simply get out. Nobody believes that.

I was in the trap. I had to act and there was no alternative. They had the red line drawn across the page under my name.

I slept again. Last thought: Pasquier had organized Ginger and friend to follow me; but who had told the professionals?

7

The invasion came before dawn. They dropped out of the sky in millions, swirling in the wind. When I left the hotel the wind had died and the city wore white. There was ten-tenths cloud cover, the clouds coming from the north-east in great grey waves like billowing poison gas.

I had never seen poison gas. My imagination was jumping.

That was normal. Images still popped in my mind: shadowed eyes in a car mirror, the glint in the basket of long loaves, the man on the fourth rung of the ladder. A car backfired and it echoed inside me, a memory of the Yamaha between the peeling walls of a narrow street.

The snow was unbelievable. Some of the cafés hadn't put the glass walls up round their terraces yet and the tables were covered in identical white cloths. I was walking down rue St-Jacques towards the Seine and the cars were stirring it into slush, traffic cops were blowing whistles at it, girls were wearing it in their hair like a Bing Crosby Christmas movie, a bunch of Africans were laughing, faces turned up to the sky, boys were inventing excuses to stay off school.

It was only the middle of November. Snow.

The front pages of the newspapers on the kiosks were crowded with photos of the Communist—Socialist rally in Clermont-Ferrand. Another headline gave the latest score in the polls: 54—46. Giscard was going to lose.

I looked towards Notre Dame and a million snowflakes were in the way. There was a café on the corner by the Petit Pont and a dumpy old waiter with a castrato voice and a striped apron rounded over his belly was calling the students *mes enfants* and shouting to the barman for *un grog*. It was for himself. Because of the cold.

And Crevecoeur's eyes were cold, I suddenly decided. His face looked compressed, and the something that had been squeezed out was human warmth. The vagueness had been deceptive, drawing attention away from the coldness of the eyes. Were they grey? No, I was imagining the ice.

I bought a coat and turned into a café for coffee. With the warm coat and the hot coffee it seemed a good day. It was just after nine o'clock and nobody had tried to kill me yet.

Nobody tried to kill me all day. I remember it for that.

The snow stopped. Girls with brooms came out to sweep paths to shop doors.

I crossed the river and picked up the 73 bus outside the Hôtel de Ville. I walked from the bridge at Neuilly, 300 metres up avenue Général de Gaulle, my eyes already on the building before I knew it was the one I wanted.

Institut 21.

It was written in black on a brushed aluminium background, a specially and expensively designed logo, a derivative of the computer typeface, thin risers and descenders suddenly swelling into the horizontal strokes of the letters.

Everything about the Institut 21 was special and expensive.

The building was a statement. It said I am going to overwhelm you with my cleverness, my uniqueness, my futuristic daring. It was a public relations exercise for the power of unlimited money. Like all public relations jobs, it told you nothing of what went on inside.

The building was round, with that one-way dark glass that gives nothing away, and I counted five storeys up. That was all I knew. Later, much later, I discovered more.

There were two entrances. One for staff had a computer check-in: you pressed in a plastic pass and faced the camera, and if the image the camera recorded wasn't syntactic with the photo in the computer's memory it spat your card back and the door remained locked. The entrance for visitors led to a reception desk with expensively designed girls, but first there were the uniformed police.

Ladouceur was missing.

I walked slowly, showing appropriate awe, past the entrance.

The final touch of grotesquerie was inset in the wall past the entrance. A notice: *Interrogez-moi. Je suis omniscient.* There was a keyboard and a computer display terminal.

56

For God's sake.

I made to walk on. But it could be useful.

As I typed on the keyboard, the question appeared on the display terminal. Pause. The answer.

Do you speak English?

Yes.

I wasn't using computer-language so how did it understand? There must be a crewcut somewhere inside the building breaking it down into the baby talk that very complex machines speak. Pasquier had implied it was the biggest brain in the world. It knew everything. Perhaps they had invented God.

Who is Director of the CIA?

Stanfield Turner.

What is the square root of minus eight?

Illogical.

Who invented the zip?

Whitcomb Judson.

What time does the Red Arrow reach Moscow?

0825.

Where is Cody?

Wyoming, USA.

Where is Ladouceur?

16bis rue de...

The computer developed desperate second thoughts and smashed over the address with a line of XXXX.

From inside the building there came a faint sound, and it resembled an alarm. I crossed the road, sheltering behind a monster carrying Danone yoghurt and watched two cops emerge.

They ran five metres out into the road, one of them blowing a whistle, the other sweeping his arms above his head. They had the aggrieved air and gestures that all police get when there's no one in sight to threaten but which the French have refined to such an art it is worth watching from a safe distance.

It started to snow again.

They were back. They wouldn't let go.

I picked the tail out as I got on the bus. He had been hanging back, engrossed in a newspaper, then jumped on the bus as if he'd only just taken in its arrival. Certainly the headline on the front page was rivetting, but he'd been immersed in the centre pages, paper masking his face.

57

He stood a little away, face turned aside. I thought I saw, reflected in the glass of the window, his eyes focus on me, but the light conditions made it impossible to be certain.

There were snowflakes on the shoulders of his coat, melting into glistening drops in the warmth of the bus. He wore a soft hat. It had a crumpled air as if it had been rolled up and stuffed into a coat pocket. If he were a streetwalker, that would be part of altering his image. His shoes had slush from walking to the bus stop, but it didn't look as if he had been hanging round in the snow. In a car, in a doorway?

The paper was the *Courrier*. He raised it, half covering the side of his face towards me. He didn't want me to recognize him again.

I could only see the end of the headline.

I wondered, because of the newspaper. Perhaps he was a reporter, camping out on the doorstep because Ladouceur was missing. A reporter would have a crumpled hat.

I couldn't make out the by-line on the newspaper story. Was it Pasquier?

But if he were a reporter he would have spoken to the police outside the Institut. They had stepped back off the road, muttering, looking round, because someone had asked the computer an indiscreet question. A reporter would have gone up and asked what the question was.

Not a reporter. Them again.

I wasn't counting but perhaps ten seconds had passed and the last passenger had got on and I moved. I didn't apologize because that's not what you do on a Paris bus: you pretend the other passengers aren't there as you make for the exit. I made the exit and I was just in time and the man with the crumpled hat and the copy of *Courrier* wasn't. It was as simple as that. He'd thought he was invisible and if he'd known I'd seen him he would have been prepared for me to break.

He forgot about shielding his face as the bus moved away. His eyes were round. He'd cut himself shaving that morning and a little tuft of cotton wool was like a snow flake on his chin.

The bus carried him away and I got a taxi. It was the first taxi that came, I wasn't playing nursery games about waiting for the third. The crumpled hat would be off at the next bus stop and running back.

The taxi-driver was one of those middle-aged Polish emigrés, with a small dog on the front passenger seat. They shared the same face. He talked. His daughter was my age—inspecting me in the mirror—and wasn't married, she was living with a man who was a studio electrician in television, did I comprehend, and now she was pregnant, and the lover was going to vote for the Communist-Socialist candidate in the election, and he arrived late for Sunday lunch because he played billiards, and it just showed, didn't it?

I replied something.

He said the fellow wore Che Guevara T-shirts and it wouldn't be so bad if only he married his daughter. I wondered why he wanted someone he so obviously disapproved of as a son-in-law.

He dropped me at Pont St-Michel and I finally got to buy a paper.

"Where's your key?"

"I must have lost it."

I had left it in the apartment. I couldn't risk going back for it.

"Lost it?" Dolbiac stood in the door, his voice rising in pitch, as if losing a key was symbolic and he was working it out. We didn't embrace. I followed him in.

There was music, little talk.

"Do you want to go out to eat?"

Outside, I felt threatened. I'd spent the afternoon in a cinema, seeing something loud, because gangsters on the screen were no threat. They didn't use real blood.

"No."

I let him go to the kitchen to prepare food. Only one person could get in at a time. The food was cold: pâté, quiche, salad. He could have heated the quiche: he was being symbolic.

His eyes were on me and I realized my glance had been going all round the room. Perhaps to him it appeared I was searching for some tell-tale trace of another woman, or saying farewell to the Bach bust, the angled chrome lamp I had given him, the provençale pot full of pencils, the pot-shard from Ephesus, the paper flower, all the litter of life. But it had been unconscious. My mind was on *Le Courrier*.

The headline: *Famous scientist flees to Russia?* It was written by Pasquier and that question mark implied uncertainty or speculation or plain untruth. I'd thought about it in the cinema, and again in this room, and I couldn't decide.

Dolbiac put Stockhausen on the record player; more symbolism. I had been known to leave the room rather than listen to Stockhausen. I hardly heard it.

There were stories from usually reliable sources that Jean-Louis Ladouceur, the brilliant young scientist missing since etc., etc., might have fled the country. It had been heard on the *grapevine* (pure Pasquier that, I could hear his tone of voice and see his flickering hands) that Ladouceur had bought a ticket to Berlin, taken the Friedrichstrasse crossing through the Wall, and boarded a plane at Schönefeld airport for Moscow. There was no explanation why Ladouceur couldn't have boarded a Moscow flight right here in Paris, but grapevines believe simple stories don't sell newspapers.

"Is he the new boy-friend?"

Dolbiac was sitting in a hard chair by the piano. My eyebrow made a question mark at him.

"You've been staring at his picture."

I had the *Courrier* on the floor where I was squatting. The front page carried a photo of Ladouceur taken during the summer at some United Nations agency conference in Geneva. It was the afternoon off, Ladouceur was in bathing trunks, there was a hotel pool, clear skies, striped umbrellas, snowy peaks in the distance. The photo had sex appeal.

"I was wondering why he should want to run away." I had almost said "defect". Military personnel, spies, politicians and scientists defect; nobody else. But the word seemed out of place; even the *Courrier* shied away from it for the moment.

"Do you know him?" Dolbiac was leaning forward in his chair.

"No."

"Like Agate. You didn't know him either. I don't understand you. Why are you so interested?"

His voice was louder, losing a grip on his emotions. Another little sign. Dolbiac was looking for a quarrel. You can fight and make up or fight and get out. I had an apartment that was probably wired and a hotel room where your soul died. I kept quiet.

And should I have had it out with him then? Asked what was the matter, confessed I was wrong, cried a little, played for sweet reconciliation? It's not my way. In any case, I don't think I was the problem. Dolbiac felt guilty because of some deception: he had simply turned the emotion into anger at me. We all do it, because it makes our inadequacies easier to live with.

I didn't answer him; my mind was too full of other men, the ones who tried to kill me. The thing about the newspaper article was this: there were still no reports about what Ladouceur had been working on, so why the assumption he had fled to Russia?

60

He wasn't concerned with defence or military research. The story was no help. It filled space with biographical details, past projects, a report from his house in Normandy (his wife refusing to talk to the press).

"I'm going to bed," Dolbiac stood up. The light from the lamp threw his shadow on the ceiling, angular and dramatic. He thought of saying something more, and left the room.

I had so little information. I knew there were Americans working in the Institut 21 under some guise. And I wondered: were they going to expose something Ladouceur was doing? But then I thought the opposite: perhaps Ladouceur was one of them, perhaps the Agency had recruited him, the Moscow rumour was part of it, and Agate hadn't liked what was coming.

I made coffee, drank it alone in the cold of the kitchen. Through the tiny square window there was a glimpse of a white roof and low clouds catching the reflected glow of the city.

Dolbiac had the light off, but he wasn't sleeping. We were each alone in the bed.

"Canuck..."

There was no response.

Then I shuddered, one of those big involuntary shudders that start at half a dozen places at once, and he put a hand out.

"Cold?"

My mind was far away, trying to recall the phrase to describe that shudder.

"Co, are you cold?"

"Yes." I needed comfort. I had remembered the expression: someone had walked on my grave.

8

I'd never met him. I'd never met his wife. But I had a ridiculous stereotype that the phrase "scientist's wife" had set up: woman with braided hair, shiny apple cheeks, two children tugging at her apron strings. Ignored by the husband, of course, but accepting it.

The computer wouldn't give Ladouceur's address but the telephone directory would: 16bis rue de Chazelles, in the

Seventeenth. It is odd how acute minds overlook the most elementary sources of information. The computer would rely on a human intelligence programming it, and the human intelligence was ordering a block on all information about Ladouceur, ignoring the information that was accessible to everyone.

There were no trips across a city full of eyes. I telephoned.

The politicians say the telephone system in France is improving, but then they would. The clicks on the line were loud.

"Hello." Man's voice.

"Is that Monsieur Ladouceur?"

"No. Who is this speaking?"

I put the receiver back. It told me all I needed. Either the line was looped into some surveillance office or they had a man physically at the rue de Chazelles address. In either case it wasn't his wife.

Now I had a choice. But I didn't want to run to Pasquier again for information.

I redialled.

"This is the Institut 21."

"The office of Chief Inspector Crevecoeur at the Sûreté. The Chief Inspector has a query for Monsieur Ladouceur's secretary."

"I'm not certain..."

I'd half expected that and the thing to do was to cut the switchboard operator short before her hesitation became fixed.

"The Chief Inspector has a tight schedule and it would be an intolerable and inexcusable waste of time going through the Minister."

"I'll pass you the duty officer."

That had always been likely too. I wondered what else. A voice announced it was Inspector Grenache.

I used nothing spectacular. The technique is elementary: they are there to refuse you permission to speak to someone, so you reverse the apparent direction of the phone call.

"This is the office of Chief Inspector Crevecoeur. Ladouceur's secretary requested permission to speak to the Chief Inspector on an important matter. This has now been cleared at political level. You are requested to instruct the switchboard to connect her, Inspector, and observe full security."

It is the formality which works, though usually there is some further check as they work out their confusion. This time I was passed through at once, which made me think Crevecoeur was more important than his rank indicated.

It was the kind of French organization where Ladouceur could have had a male secretary. But it was a young woman and she sounded worried and I changed the story. I worked at Samaritaine and the girl in garden leisure had gone on honeymoon and I couldn't read the writing in the order book and I was desolated to trouble her but it would save me from getting into hot water and on and on.

She interrupted: What was it?

Oh, it was the barbecue Monsieur Ladouceur ordered a fortnight ago, it was in stock now but the address of his house in Normandy was illegible, *mauvaise affaire* when the department manager found out it hadn't been despatched. The role-playing was so convincing that I found my face set in anxiety lines when I got what I wanted.

It was in a village near Clécy in the department of Calvados.

It was no day for driving. It was 250 kilometres, with the big trucks throwing slush on my windscreen and middle-aged men in Peugeots in a hurry to get somewhere, the casualty ward no doubt. I took the N13, cutting south-west before Caen, until I joined up with the D562. In summer there would be fields of maize and sugar-beet. Now there was snow. They call the region *la Suisse normande,* no alpine peaks, but soft green pastures and pine trees along the river Orne. There was a lot of new building, stucco beginning to weather, the Germans having contested every village in bitter fighting in 1944.

I bought bread and ham and a bottle of milk and sat in the car with a view down to a great loop of the river. There were a score of cows, brown and white, standing in the snow. But the milk tasted as if it were made in a factory in Lille.

The clouds broke and the sun came out, sparkling on the new snow. It was welcome, even it if wouldn't last long, for sun is always optimistic. I sat and built theories, and in the end felt reasonably satisfied.

This was the last moment when it seemed simple.

Construction: Agate worked for the Central Intelligence Agency (it could have been the National Security Agency, the Defence Intelligence Agency, Army Intelligence, Pentagon Special Operations, even the FBI, but I reasoned he would have specified if it were anything but CIA: people outside the CIA are eager to have the fact known). He was pushed into a covert operation he couldn't stomach. He knew of no disinterested organization he could turn to, but he half knew of me: no crusader, but I had rebelled before him. He wanted to tell me because I might help. He hadn't reckoned on Duraine and McKosker being ruthless enough to kill one of their own gone astray. His information was about Ladouceur's disappearance. Two possibilities: the Agency had kidnapped Ladouceur, or Ladouceur was also CIA and had gone to earth.

My construction wasn't complete. I didn't know what Ladouceur's work was or what his disappearance would achieve. But Ladouceur's wife might help. If I knew, I could take some sort of action. Then there'd be no reason to keep sending hit teams after me.

I crossed the bridge and left the car in the centre of the village.

A man was shaking snow off the bowed branches of a blue pine and he directed me down a track parallel with the river. A line of aspens on the bank was naked and cold. There were more cows standing in the snow, uncertain what to do, full of cream and gentleness. There were wild blackberry canes and doves wheeling above a farmhouse, and in summer you'd want to lie down in the long grass and remember childhood.

I could see the tiled roof of the house through apple trees that must have been sixty years old. The last time I had been in Normandy the trees had been drifting down petals like snow; with the real stuff blanketing everything, the image seemed banal. I went through an iron gate and as I passed a big bed of irises, green sword leaves piercing the white, there was the voice.

"*Ne bougez pas, ne bougez pas.*"

It was very urgent.

Two things happened. I froze. I froze absolutely still. And the animal came at me, bursting through some evergreen bushes.

"*Ne bougez pas*", the voice had said. You don't use the formal *vouvoyer* on an animal. The command had been intended for me and I hoped it had been given by someone who was certain of the animal's behaviour pattern or I would be dead.

There are not many dogs that provoke fear in me. Some people are terrified by the Alsatian, but it's not fundamentally aggressive, only by conditioning. I'd rather face an Alsatian than a Komondor, which looks like a snowy mountain; Hungarian shepherds use it to protect their flocks against the wolves. The Komondor is a killer. It can cut down a wolf or bear with ease; a human has no chance. I would keep clear of a bull mastiff; it has the pugnacity of the old bearbaiting bulldog and the power to keep a strong man pinned to the ground for hours. And then there's this one.

64

The Doberman Pinscher was accelerating as it turned up the path towards me, shoulder muscles bunching and stretching under the blue-black coat. It was fully grown and had its adult strength.

Only my eyes moved.

When a dog charges it is useless to try and run. You stand your ground and kick to catch the animal in the throat, hope to break the windpipe, and even if you misjudge its speed you'll hit something. The dog's lips are very sensitive. It's one of those concepts that is easier to believe on the training ground with a dog that is muzzled and wears a training collar.

It neither barked nor growled. Even with the snow muffling sound, I could hear its claws disturbing loose stones. It was desperate to get at me.

The dog was less than half my weight, but it had momentum. I would be lucky to get one kick and it would be on me.

My eyes dropped as the distance between us narrowed.

"Dobie, stop!"

In time.

It looked in my face from a distance of two metres. Its head was a blunt wedge, flat, with its ears cropped. It had rust markings above the eyes, jaw dropped, tongue slipping over the canines.

It was a male and they're not so easy to train as bitches, but this one was under the total control of the person I could not see.

I did not probe the trees or the windows of the house to search out the owner of the voice. My eyes were steady on his. The Doberman can have a streak of vicious meanness and it's better to lock your gaze so your moving eyes don't provoke him.

A breeze came from the north, drifting snow from the apple trees in my direction. He would not smell my fear.

"Qu'est-ce que vous cherchez, vous là-bas?"

I wasn't searching for a fight with twenty-five kilos of muscle and bone. The full-grown Doberman has forty-two teeth and if he goes for your throat it's hopeless. I'd seen one take a kid trying to make for the Wall in East Berlin. There are mines and the Vopos have automatic rifles, but it was the Doberman that got him. You have to be suicidal to try and hop the Wall, and it's not much better going any other way. I know. I've been.

The Doberman had knocked the boy down and gone for the throat. He was, perhaps, sixteen or seventeen though his face looked older with his mouth distorted in a scream. He had put an arm up to shield his throat and the dog had moved up to the face. He savaged the boy's eyes and nose and wrists, and then returned to the jugular. There was red everywhere. It was ugly, like the way the Vopos had done nothing. There was nothing the Vopos could do because the dogs are trained to attack any human in the zone by the Wall. Vopos try to escape too. Finally there had been just the sound of teeth worrying flesh.

"Stay, Dobie, stay."

English words. And the voice American, a woman's, coloratura.

"Your dog Dobie," I said. "Is it safe if I move my head?"

"The head's okay. Not your body, particularly not your hands."

I very much wanted to move my hands to massage the tenseness out of the neck muscles. I eased my head from side to side and looked for the woman.

"Why have you come here?" she shouted.

"Not to outface a Doberman."

The voice came from the single pine tree that was planted, French style, in the centre of the lawn in front of the house. She was behind, I couldn't see her.

"He's all right. He's my protection."

He'd be protection enough. There was little you could do to stop the dog unless you got him in your rifle sights before he knew you were there. A handgun would be no use. Knife maybe, if you wanted to risk closing with him. Protection against what? It was all peace and quiet, just the sound of a cow away in the meadow by the river.

"Who are you?" she asked.

"My name's Cody. You're Ladouceur's wife?"

"Who the shit are you, Cody?"

I saw her then. There was anger in her voice and she made a movement. The sombreness of the branches of the pine had masked her. She was all black, not only skin but clothes: black sweater, black slacks. Nobody had told me Ladouceur's wife was American.

"You know J-L? You some kind of girl-friend?"

"J-L?"

"My husband."

"I've never met him."

"Then what do you want here?"

"I can't talk like this, you hiding behind a tree, the dog ready..."

"You talk."

The voice had a rasp that couldn't have been her normal tone.

It affected the dog and he growled very low, his hindquarters trembling. It wouldn't take much to trigger him.

"A few days ago a man came to see me. I'd never met him before. He was desperate about something, but before he could tell me, he was killed. I think he wanted to warn me about a plot against your husband. He's disappeared, hasn't he?"

"Do they know?"

I didn't understand the question. It felt wrong.

"Why have you come?"

The pause had only been fractional.

I said: "The man who was killed seemed to think I could do something to stop it."

"What are you? Some kind of private investigator trying to hustle up a contract?"

The voice grated again; it was the voice of someone living close to the abyss. Her nerves could snap and she'd be over the edge with no safety net. The Doberman would think I'd pushed.

"I'm trying to save my life. Whoever snatched your husband, if he has disappeared, thinks I know something. They've tried to kill me twice."

Then I made the error.

I raised a hand, a gesture at the memory of the rifle glinting among the long loaves, and the dog took it wrong.

There was no command from the woman, no snarl from the dog. I had a fraction of a second's warning as his eyes shifted from my moving hand to my throat and he braced his rear legs. No logical sequence went through my brain, though there must have been some selection process that decided I didn't just continue raising the hand to protect my windpipe.

The teeth. Above all I had to guard against them.

It was the ultimate in sacrifice throws since I would end up defenceless, on my back, on the ground. All I would gain was four or five seconds, hope that the woman would reassert control.

In contest conditions it would not have been recognized as a classic *tomoenage*. But when you're fighting a Doberman you improvise. I bent my knees as the dog came through the air, reached out both hands to grasp him at the top of his front legs under his shoulders. His jaws were open but there was no instant to worry about that as I squatted back, putting my right foot in his stomach and rolled backwards on the ground. I straightened my leg, lifting him as high as I could, which would undoubtedly have lost me the judge's approval. I wanted to kick him clear and

I was not concerned whether he was hurt, only with achieving the longest interval before he turned back. He made a half-turn in the air, landed on his neck and shoulders a couple of metres beyond. It should have been further for an opponent of that weight but my grip slipped on his smooth coat.

The shrill yelp would be surprise not injury. I could hear the nails of his paws scrambling for a purchase on the frozen path.

She came out from behind the tree, shouting and thank God she'd trained the dog well. Even in the middle of a rough-house it stopped, looking away to her, and I got to my feet.

"Jesus, I never seen anyone do that to a dog."

Jesus, nor had I.

"Heel, Dobie." She turned and made for the house.

The Doberman didn't like me. He sat in a corner of the room, head raised, and the eyes above the flat cheeks locked on me with coldness. I could move because she'd told the dog I was a friend. The dog didn't believe her, and who could blame him. I didn't believe it myself.

It wasn't easy.

I'd followed her in without being asked and sat where I could see both woman and dog without moving my head. I was shaken by the attack but I didn't want to show nerves in front of either. It wasn't pride on my part. They were both too strung up. Bear in mind the causes and you had to make allowance for her stress: missing husband, media interest, probably police.

She didn't speak at first. She sat on the edge of a hard chair, hands gripping her knees, tendons in the neck prominent, face closed and at an angle to me. I didn't know what she thought of me, what I did, why I was there. I hardly knew why I was there myself except I had the idea it might save my life.

If she weren't talking, I was going to have to put questions and I didn't know what to ask.

I asked her name. I couldn't think of her as Madame Ladouceur.

"Dee."

One of those names like Skip or Credo or Oz that you don't know whether the parents gave or the kids at school or whether it's the family name or even whether it's boy or girl. A today name. It might as well be a number, but that's a tomorrow name.

"Have you been married to him long?"

It was a personal sort of question but how else to prime her into the habit of talking? She moved her head a little towards me and echoed "Married?", as if she weren't married to him or maybe meaning what business was it of mine.

"He's thirty-two, isn't he? I read it in the paper."

"Yeah."

A child can never estimate an adult's age. I have a similar disability with a black woman. It is something to do with the bone structure making the face smoother. Twenty-four, twenty-five? There were lines on her forehead but they were the surface ripples of the whirlpool inside.

"Do you have any family?"

She blinked, my presence registering more.

"No, no kids."

I hadn't thought so, not with the Doberman. It was her dog not his, her training, her voice it responded to, her language. It was her substitute for a family. Another thing, the Doberman is held to have an affectionate nature in the home among those it knows. But for all that it can be temperamental and react badly to the unthinking knocks of a small child.

She was breathing deeply but at long intervals. Her face was clouded.

"Did you meet Jean-Louis at college?"

Finally she broke. The eyes jerked at me.

"College? Listen sister, I went to Fuck U, what they call the college of life."

That was better.

When the first stone slips in the dam wall, the water comes in a trickle. But you can't stop it. It picks at rocks, carries them away, while you watch the trickle grow to a current, a torrent, the dam wall crumbling and finally the pent-up weight of water sweeping the whole structure away.

She'd kept it inside because there was no one to tell it to. You can speak to the sky or the dog or the mirror, but it's no substitute for another human presence. That's why half-believers like Dolbiac keep going to confession: it's not insurance, it's because there's another person on the other side of the wooden grille when you bring out your petty lusts and hates.

It came in phrases, repetitions, back tracks, half sentences, gaps I filled in myself.

Ghetto child, seventh of nine, smell of blood, father a carcass dresser in Chicago, Saturday nights his eyes had the stunned look the cattle had during the week, booze, another woman, another quarrel, shouting and going and coming back, mother defeated, cold water apartment, three flights up and no one swept the used rubbers from the corners of the landings where the light sockets hung empty, when she was eleven her brother three years older had her in the dirt in one of those corners, one of Daley's truncheon boys cracked her father's skull in 1968, needle-marks in her arm, she could dance a little, strip a little, hustle a little, cold streets, cold eyes, rolling a drunk, night in the lock-up, warder with Four Roses on his breath and a wart on his dickey wanting a blow job but she bit instead, four years in the Correctional Establishment and she got out two days before her twentieth birthday.

I've set it down rough because that's how it came out. She didn't give her story big production values because her life never had any.

The Doberman sat tense while she talked, distressed by the pain and anger in her voice. She was rigid in the chair, I don't think she knew who I was, just a human presence. Tears were the physical counterpart to the emotional dam sweeping away.

"It was July when I met J-L. July is hot in Chicago and I was high. I'd been stoned since thirty minutes after I walked out those big gates. I'd been swallowing a great big technicolour cocktail. Bluebirds and Speedballs and Brownies and Dexies and Red Devils and Blockbusters. I'd schmecked some and I was popping again. I'd had a dirty needle and some crook doctor was on my back. Brought me round, gave me stuff, just do a trick for him Sunday afternoons while his wife went to visit with her mother. Four months of Sunday afternoons I don't remember."

She pushed up a sleeve of the black sweater. The skin near the inside of the elbow was pitted like a slice of pumpernickel. There was a pink stain in the skin the size of her thumbnail.

"They don't heal. When I go to the beach and strip, people stare and stare. I'm a marked person."

She held her hand out, and it was steady.

"Finished now. Only the scars don't heal."

It was taking a long time. But we each have to exorcise our devils in our own way.

"I had three months to live, three weeks, three hours, there's no telling. Boys push, girls hustle. Sooner or later there's some hophead who's clawing for it and can't pay you and you shake hands with a knife. Listen, there were some blocks where the police *cars* even went in pairs in case one stalled."

I just listened. There were scars I could see and scars I couldn't.

"It got desperate. The doctor went on vacation. I had this Saturday night special, cheap job I'd lifted from the inside pocket of some john. Early evening I went into a liquor store and the man wasn't ready for the idea that some girl was going to come in waving a shooter and dip in the cash drawer. He reached under the counter and I squeezed and he made so much noise going back into the shelves of tequila and Puerto Rican cane juice, I got scared. I ran."

She was restless with the memory and walked to the window, the dog's eyes following her. There was a narrow terrace outside with metal chairs and a table and some stone troughs with geraniums dying in the snow. It would be a marvellous place to sit after a big July day and share a bottle of cold Muscadet. She looked out but she was seeing something else.

"I ran two blocks and nobody tried to stop me. You stop someone and you get involved. I ran out of legs and was bumping against the wall of a building. It was brick. I remember the roughness against my cheek. He came out of the doorway and put his arm round me. I thought it was just whitey wanting to screw a black girl. That was my last thought."

She stopped. She stayed silent so long I thought there was going to be no more. I made a small movement, mindful of the Doberman.

"I woke up and it was his hotel room. His face kept circling above me and I was sweating and cursing him for getting me in his bed. One minute I was yelling and the next vomiting down the front of my T-shirt. I was sobbing and shouting and the sick was coming green out of my nose. I was hot and shaking and he took a razor to my T-shirt. He gave me his pyjamas and then the doctor came, a friend of J-L's from the conference, and they talked in French. I didn't understand. Just as well. The doctor was explaining to J-L what cold turkey meant. He saved my life. Not the doctor."

Dee sat down again. She stared.

"You don't know him, do you?"

"No."

"He's a good man. Remember that."

There was an expression on her face, like: Whatever happens, hold on to that fact.

"You don't know what I mean." Her voice had a shading to it, pity for the outsider. "I don't mean a holy angel. Just plain good. You don't meet that kind of man. He saved my life because he ran into me and became involved. He gave a damn when nobody else did. He was interested. People, the world, ideas. He wanted to know about everything and everyone. Listen, he was there for this international conference and he got talking to the doorman about old Chicago jazz, I don't know what, about whether Frank Melrose was a better pianist than Joe Sullivan, that kind of stuff. As a kid the doorman used to hang round the clubs and he'd heard the old bands. He had some scratchy 78s and J-L went round to his rooming house, whitey in the ghetto on Saturday night. That's when I ran into him. He pulled me out. He was taking a vacation after the conference but he couldn't leave me on my own. He knew I wouldn't come out the other side. He took a cabin up towards Black River and he lived on whiskey and I lived on cold turkey. You know cold turkey? The whole of you is screaming for it and sometimes you yell, sometimes you beg and cry, sometimes you're sneaky, sometimes you fight. It was no vacation for him. Don't ask me about it."

She wiped at her cheeks, angry to find there were still tears there.

"When he flew back to Paris, I was on the plane with him. Some alley cat he'd known four weeks. He had this apartment in rue de Chazelles and we had separate bedrooms for two months. Maybe he wanted to clean me up first but he never made it seem that way. I began eating, no junk, a little red wine, we went to the country for week-ends, made me ride a bicycle. He started teaching me French, took me out, made me read. He created me."

She stopped again. "I don't think so," I said. "You were there all the time. He just brushed the soil from on top."

She looked at me a long time. "That's the way he'd see it. He said it was capitalist society that formed failures."

You can always explain it away. You can be out of a job or have a job that destroys you. You can be poor or be rich to boredom. You can be godless or be suffocated by the Church's restrictions. Take your choice. Ladouceur was a marxist and human shortcomings were the result of the system. Never mind there were more drunks in Warsaw than in Chicago, he'd explain that away too.

I asked: "What are his friends like?"

"All sorts. No one special."

Could be true, could be shielding. She was taking her time with the answers now.

"Perhaps he needed you as much as you needed him."

"He was no hermit. He knew a thousand people, to go to a restaurant, go to the cinema, to argue. If I gave him something more, well, that's why he married me."

Was, knew, gave. The past tense, as if he were past, it was an obituary. There was something else that had been lying at the back of my mind and it had been itching itself forward. But I didn't want to ask directly. She'd have to bring it up herself.

"When did you get this place?"

"Couple of years back. Dobie too, to look after me when I'm alone."

"Surely there's no danger here?"

No answer.

"You stay here all the time he's in Paris?"

"He comes down at week-ends. I keep busy. I teach class in Clécy three mornings. Spoken English. Me, a teacher. You should have heard me four years ago."

"When did he last come down?"

"Two week-ends ago."

"And?"

"And nothing."

It wasn't quite enough. She'd been worried, tense, but now she'd got over the flush of confession and was drying up. It wasn't that I didn't believe the ghetto and the pick-up. But there were little things.

"You've no idea where he is?"

"No."

"He gave no hint of anything wrong?"

"No."

"I'm surprised there's no police guard."

"I've got Dobie." She clicked her fingers and the dog went to her at once. She stroked its head. "The police came."

"Who? The Sûreté?"

She thought about it, though she must have known. "Yes. Asked the usual damn fool questions about girls and blackmail and mental illness."

"Did they ask if he was worried about work?"

"Sure, they wanted to know all about his work. I told what I knew. J-L had been working on the Algerian project and now there was oil-from-coal."

I waited, because I got the impression she had stopped herself.

"Could you tell *me* what he was doing?"

She snapped her face up. "What I told the cops. The oil-from-coal project, nothing more."

"He wasn't working for anybody else?" I put it as neutrally as I could and she didn't react at first, and then I could see her stiffen and I was worried because the Doberman tensed as well.

"Spit it out, Cody."

"There's a rumour he was working on some hush contract."

She stared and her hand stopped fondling the Doberman's head.

"Seems you know a hell of a lot more than you let on."

The shutters came down.

There was snow again, like confetti. I was feeling colder.

Do they know?

She'd used the phrase, and then caught herself. It had worried me at the time but I'd put it aside because there were more pressing problems. Did who know? About Ladouceur, Agate, me?

I walked past cows and bare trees and decided the snow wasn't like confetti. God was giving a tickertape welcome to winter.

And the other thing. The police had made inquiries about him, possible motives for vanishing. But queries about girls and so forth were a blind.

They wanted to check what she knew of his projects, his contacts, any trigger for a possible defection. She'd hesitated when she told me. She was uneasy.

9

I found out why the police had left Dee Ladouceur on her own.
    They hadn't.

He was sitting in my car, though I'd locked it, watching through a tiny patch of clear windscreen as I came down the street. He shifted over to the passenger seat when I went round to the driving side. The door was still locked as though he wanted me to think he'd pulled a clever trick materializing inside a locked car. I fiddled with a key and he watched, smoking a cigarette.

I slid on to the seat and wound down the window to let out some of the grey air.

"*Quatorze juillet-La Bastille. Ladouceur—softness.*" He nodded his head in his vague way but his eyes were steady enough. "You were holding out on me."

"I was holding out?" The surprise in my voice must have sounded genuine for Crevecoeur's eyebrows rose.

"You pretended you knew nothing about Ladouceur."

"I didn't know anything. You put the idea in my mind. I didn't want to get involved. Everyone else wanted to involve me: you, Agate, the others."

"The others?" He was casual, as if I'd made a slip but he didn't want to show he'd caught me at it. I didn't care. I was angry, with him, with the woman I'd just seen, with the dog that had jumped me, with the people who'd got me in their sights.

"The ones who tried to kill me."

"That is serious. Why didn't you report it to the police?"

"What would you have done?"

"Investigated."

"How do you investigate an election rally or a dozen men haunting a public garden?"

"That isn't the point. It helps our understanding, fills in the picture. It is your duty as a citizen."

"I'm not a citizen."

"Of course, I was forgetting; you are a foreigner with a *carte de séjour* that needs renewing."

We ran headlong into silence. I filled time by wiping condensation off the windscreen. I saw a fellow in a beret come out of the Café des Sports, shake hands with a man getting off a Mobylette, and they went back in the café. Someone had written in red paint on a wall, *VOTEZ COMUNISTE*, and then messed it up trying to add the missing M. It was a long message to paint on a wall but it was the kind of village where you wouldn't be disturbed after dark. The kind of village where you had to be very frightened to need to keep a Doberman.

"Do you mind telling me how you found out about the house here?"

"I'm not stupid."

"No," he said. He gave me his vague look and tried again. "What is your opinion of Mme Ladouceur?"

"Sharp, scared of something, hiding something. What do you think of her?"

"Me?" It was obviously improper to question a Chief Inspector. "Sharp, scared of something, hiding something. Possibly dangerous."

75

The schoolkid sticks his tongue out behind the teacher's back. The mechanic drops the oilcan in the lathe when the foreman turns away. We react against authority, each in our own way.

So I asked: "What were you doing when you were in America, working for SDECE?"

A sharpness came in his eyes, displacing the vague air. The French pronounce it as if it were an Italian word, but SDECE is French through and through: Service de Documentation Extérieure et de Contre-Espionage. Its image is tarnished, like the Agency's, and no one admits working for it. His look passed and he took a breath. It was obviously being another of those difficult days.

"I was responsible for security in the embassy building in Washington. Does that satisfy you?"

I shrugged. Somebody has to be responsible for embassy security, but it is rather like saying you work in the visa section: you can do anything just so long as the ambassador doesn't have his nose rubbed in the dirt.

"All right. You want me to be good and promise not to see Ladouceur's wife again. If there's nothing else, you might let me get back to Paris."

He didn't move. I waited for it to come, and when it did it wasn't what I expected.

"What do you know about Ladouceur?" he asked.

"Nothing. He's a scientist, rumoured to have some hush assignment, and he's missing."

He finished his cigarette and made his decision. He leaned across me to wind up the window. "You never know," he said. He had a smile that lasted a couple of seconds and added more vertical lines to his long compressed face. Then he started to speak, staring fixedly ahead like a newscaster reading off the autocue.

"I was working at the embassy in Washington at the time of the Chicago Conference on Marine Technology, four and a half years ago. There are dozens of these conferences going on all the time, the principal reason being that attendance at them is tax-deductible, though I don't know who should want to go sightseeing in Chicago. But this one was a little unusual and Paris had asked for somebody from the embassy to go up and keep an eye on it. The Institut 21 had only recently been set up. Our government was anxious to impress the Third World countries, and sent its most brilliant young scientist as a member of the delegation. Ladouceur was *un succès fou*. He was twenty-seven, twenty-eight.

76

Handsome. Undeniably brilliant. Boundless energy, going to parties, discussion groups, sparking with ideas, so on. And he had what you Americans call radical chic. About half-way through the conference he delivered a remarkable, no, a stunning paper on Iceships. That is, ocean-going ships that are constructed out of frozen water. Don't say it's impossible."

He glanced at me. I hadn't intended to say anything. I was too worried by these sudden confidences.

"Water has some remarkable properties; among them is the fact that when frozen it is one of the hardest substances and yet it floats. Ladouceur had the idea of taking the base material for newsprint, wood-pulp, mixing it with eight times its volume of water, and freezing it. The result is a frozen solid mass some four or five times as rigid as concrete, thanks to the ice and the structure of the hemi-cellulose of the wood fibre, and difficult to melt because of its insulating effects. You've seen *clochards* wrapped in newspaper on the métro gratings?"

I didn't need the science lecture, modified for idiots. I needed a friend, I needed a holiday, someplace hot. I was worried because before he'd been concerned to keep me ignorant, and now he was concerned to involve me. That's the time to be frightened of security police.

"Ladouceur had constructed a model in ice/wood-pulp. It didn't even feel very cold to the touch. The full-scale ship would have a refrigeration plant circulating cold air round the hull. In moderately cold waters it would be very economical to run. He should have given us advance notice of what he was going to say because it caused a sensation. Water being free, the Iceship is cheaper to construct than conventional metal hulls. And there are military implications: if the hull is made extremely thick, say seven metres, a mine or torpedo won't penetrate it, simply gouge a pocket. It can be repaired at sea by refreezing more wood-pulp. Apart from nuclear attack it is difficult to sink."

"You actually saw the model?"

"Yes."

"Why are you telling me?" I had to know.

"Just a minute. The delegates were fascinated, especially the ones with cold water shipping, the Scandinavians, Canada and the Soviet Union. Very cheap to manufacture where the climate is already cold and there's an abundance of wood-pulp and hydro-electricity for freezing. Two days after delivering his paper,

Ladouceur literally bumped into a desperate drug-ridden woman who collapsed in his arms. Did she tell you?"

"Yes."

"Happy chance, wasn't it."

We sat and watched a body in a shapeless blue coat walk past the car, basket on arm. The basket had a cauliflower on top, creating the illusion that snow had got in.

No professional likes chance. Chance is what you can't guard against. Worse, if you believe in chance you become a fatalist, your brain no longer asks who and why and how.

I asked: "Have you checked her?"

Crevecoeur made that Gallic movement which is as much sinking the head down as shrugging the shoulders.

"We ran a trace. Certainly Dee Forrest existed, daughter of a meat dresser in a Chicago abattoir, imprisoned for assault on a prison officer, drug addict, etc. So?"

"She showed me the needle scars," I said. "She sounded absolutely real."

"All that could be one hundred per cent genuine, and yet not be all the truth. Such a brilliant man, such a tempting target."

Nobody gives the whole truth. Crevecoeur wasn't giving me the whole truth about Ladouceur and his wife. He was being much more effective: giving me selected facts and letting my imagination go to work. If he'd flatly said that Dee Ladouceur (née Forrest) was a Soviet spy or an American spy, I'd have protested. But how do you protest against your imagination?

"What do you want from me?" He had a reason, might even give it to me.

"It's three days since Agate was murdered. First they tried to eliminate you. Now I think they'll want to find out how much you've discovered, who you're working for."

"Nobody."

He smiled. It was narrower than before. It said: I may believe you when a thousand others wouldn't.

"I don't want anything from you," he said, "except you should tell me of any meeting with them."

"Who are they?"

"Well now, you tell me."

I think Crevecoeur enjoyed his job. The window was steamed up again. He cleaned it, peered ahead and turned to me.

"Also, it is only fair to warn you. You're a beautiful woman. If I see you naked, I don't want it to be on a cart in the police

78

mortuary. After I identify the body it would be slid back into one of the cold chambers, chilled to three degrees, kept until after the legal *procès*, and then cremated."

He got out of the car and walked down the street in the direction of a dark blue Renault 16. I kept waiting for him to turn back to deliver a final punch line.

He was saving it.

I had trouble with the car and for a time I wondered if Crevecoeur had sabotaged it. I had coffee in the Café des Sports while the mechanic from the garage in Clécy poked round. I could see him scratching his body and eventually he fetched his tow-truck and pumped a charge through to the battery. He fetched me out and said there was a short-circuit and it needed a thorough check, but I said it could wait. I had lost an hour.

I crossed the Orne, and it was just before the *route nationale* that I came on the roadblock, flashing light on the police car, barriers, spidermen on shiny 750 cc BMWs. The uniformed man checked my number plate, my driving licence and my face, and I knew how Bonnie felt. I was given celebrity treatment, motorbikes front and rear, traffic clearing at our siren.

Dark was settling in early because of the cloud cover.

I was escorted to a small hotel on a crossroads, neat white shutters, last red leaves clinging to the virginia creeper. Inside, Crevecoeur again.

"You took your time." The line of tension was deep between his eyes. "I have a phone call to make. Wait here." Here was a small sitting room off the bar with a uniformed man at the door to keep intruders out, me in.

When Crevecoeur returned he nodded to me and told the cop to go home.

"What sort of game are you playing?" I couldn't even feel very angry.

"War games," he said, and thought about it a bit. "Cold War games."

"God," I said.

"Don't despise Cold War games," he said. "They're the alternative to World War Three." There was some lukewarm coffee in a cup and he drained it. "I'm sorry if I've been pushing you round." Then he added, "Don't think that was an apology." He would never admit to being wrong.

"Nobody tells me anything."

"I felt it necessary to test you. I wanted to see if, after I'd spoken to you, you made a report to Mme Ladouceur. It was conceivable you might have been a contact with her. I was worried when you were such a long time getting on the road but I checked with Clécy, you're clean."

"Thank you."

"Don't thank me too much. You're only clean in that you've no adverse connections in this situation."

There was a pause. Crevecoeur was a good Intelligence man, knowing how to make the unsaid things speak. He wouldn't be blatant about my residence papers again.

"I have to admit," he went on, "you make me curious. Why are you involved in this?"

"People keep on trying to kill me. I'm protecting myself. That is my involvement."

Truth is a poor advocate to people like Crevecoeur.

"Others would go to the police, or at worst leave the country, because they would be frightened and incompetent. You are neither."

He had his head on one side to watch me.

"Now, it would be easy to have you deported." he said. "But why should I? You have involved yourself, or others have involved you, and you have your uses."

Finally he'd come to it.

Freelances are useful, though no outfit admits to using them. If anything goes sour with a freelance, everything is capable of being denied. Take a random letter: C. Think of the countries beginning with C. Think of the denials all sides make of being involved: Congo, Cyprus, Chile, Cambodia, Cuba. The Agency has even formalized this with a Denial Capability Rating, ranging from zero to ten. The higher DCR a covert operation scores, the better. Freelances, being totally deniable, score very high DCRs. If Crevecoeur didn't want to risk annoying another country, or more important annoying another country's Intelligence organization, a freelance was the figleaf. And in my case he didn't even have to recruit, I was already in deep.

"There's no money involved," he said. "I wouldn't want to compromise you with the tax authorities."

Another pause. He was letting me work it all out.

"I've booked us rooms at the hotel tonight. I don't think you should drive back. The roads aren't safe, Paris even less so. I

80

should be honoured if you would let me buy you dinner. The chef here is really very good."

He gave me a smile as wide as a mousetrap.

"Tell me about your visit to your friend Pasquier," he said.

"There's nothing to tell," I said. "I got a little background on Ladouceur and the Institut 21."

Crevecoeur was testing again, this time whether I could work it all out from his one remark. He'd known I'd visited Pasquier, therefore was Pasquier one of his men? No, because in that case he would never have used amateurs like Ginger to follow me. Then how had he known? I hadn't been tailed to Pasquier, but obviously I had been tailed away. Not just by the amateurs, with whom I'd been preoccupied, but by the professionals whom I'd not picked out till later. The professionals must have had Pasquier under observation.

"Two things," I said. "One: tell your men next time they follow me into a jazz cellar I shan't just run away up a ladder. Two: tell me why you're watching Pasquier."

"I think," Crevecoeur said, "well have a Pouilly-Fumé to start with. Crab has quite a sweet flesh, after all, and Chablis might be too dry but Sancerre not quite dry enough." And then, in a tone of voice as if it were no more important, "You would never have picked them out if they hadn't climbed the barrier to the platform."

"They didn't," I said.

"At the next station, I meant."

"They didn't," I repeated.

"It was when you were preoccupied, talking to the young man with the red hair."

"No," I said. "That wasn't until the train was moving again. Now stop treating me like a young pup in the first week at training camp."

He gave me the dents at the corners of his mouth that were his narrow smile. He'd tested me on deduction, tested me three times on observation, and I'd passed. "They telephoned to the next station and the train waited a minute. You might have noticed except..."

"If I got neurotic every time the métro waited in Paris..." It was my turn to let a sentence die.

Crevecoeur tucked his napkin in his shirt collar. I'd never eaten dinner with a man who did that. I thought only fat Belgians did it, and then only in cartoons. When he set to work cracking the crab's shell and sucking the flesh from each leg, I saw it had been a defensive measure.

"Pasquier." Crevecoeur was a true product of the French educational system. Everything was itemized, arranged in order, given its subheading; and the little lecture commenced. "It's instructive that Pasquier is the one who's broken every story about Ladouceur. He has written general articles on Ladouceur's work, he reported Ladouceur missing first, he speculated on Ladouceur's possible flight to the Soviet Union. Now what does that tell you?"

He didn't want me to answer.

"It's obvious: Pasquier is being fed. Somebody, somewhere, has a plan that involves the disappearance of a brilliant young scientist and is leaking the story piece by piece to Pasquier. We can't find anything in his apartment, his telephone calls have been either to do with other stories or have had, how shall I say, an erotic content. But he is somebody's mouthpiece, witting or unwitting."

"You don't think it's possible Ladouceur is a plain and simple defector?" I'd finally used the word. I shouldn't have.

"What is this nonsense about 'defecting'?"

I've had men stare at me over their wine glass before but not with that kind of look. "If Ladouceur wishes to take his brain and donate it to the Moscow Academy of Science, he is perfectly free to do so. Do not confuse individual rights in France, or even in America, with those in the Eastern bloc. He can think, talk, live and work how he pleases. There is no question of defection. Unless he has committed a criminal act, he is free to go. You know that perfectly well. So if he hasn't disappeared for that reason, and it's not for another woman or amnesia, why has he? Think about it."

And then there were puff pastry boats with little black *morilles* staining the cream sauce, and then guinea fowl with *pommes souflées*. Crevecoeur ordered some Pauillac, I never saw the label, and he remarked on the bouquet like violets and the complex succession of tastes on the palate.

"That's because of the congenerics," I said.

He looked at me: I was an uncouth American.

We talked of other things, nothing personal, nothing of consequence, except I made the mistake of a glancing reference to de Gaulle.

"De Gaulle." Crevecoeur made another little subheading, but then he cancelled the lecture. All I got was: "When politicans make errors on a truly heroic scale, one no longer sees the mistakes and the politician becomes a statesman."

I ended with an unadorned pear, which Crevecoeur approved of.

"Thank you for dinner," I said, even if it were the French tax-payer who should be thanked.

"There's no such thing as a free dinner," he said, as if I needed reminding.

Coffee. No, I wouldn't have cognac.

"The security set-up in France." He made a gesture as if underscoring the subheading. "It is more complicated than in any other country in the world. I work for the Sûreté Nationale but I feel quite lonely when I consider all the others there are. SDECE of course, the Africa Bureau, the Bureau for the Development of Agriculture, the Deuxième Bureau, Direction de la Surveillance du Territoire, three separate military organizations. Then the President has set up his own outfit: Salut Spécial, which we are forbidden to refer to by its initial letters. They all have one thing in common: they are riddled from top to bottom by informers and agents. I know one member of the cabinet who is a Soviet agent, many officers at high levels in all the security organizations who report to Moscow. Even, which would have made de Gaulle still angrier, agents who report to Washington. The point is: it is impossible to mount any kind of concerted security operation because when you make a raid the files are empty or the contact never turns up at the drop point. One can only act solo. That is why I am so certain you will be of assistance to me."

"Because I'm outside in the cold on my own," I said.

"No, no. I sent an internal memo saying you were co-operating with me. So they'll no longer want to kill you, they'll be clustering like wasps at a jam jar. They'll be after your life story."

The waiter came with the pot.

"Your coffee's getting cold," Crevecoeur said.

He was French to the end. He escorted me to my bedroom door and asked if there was anything more I needed.

There'd be a subheading for that.

10

There is a kind of brittle wit you get at parties in the First arrondissement. A man with the regulation drooping moustache and eyes that looked past my shoulder had said: "Never trust any organization with three initials: ITT, IBM, FBI, CIA and particularly USA." He was pleased with himself because it was at a party given by an American (it had been J). He poured himself some more Scotch and moved to find someone else to insult.

I was not prejudiced. I didn't want any set of letters after me: KGB, CIA, SN, SDECE, DST or the French President's SS.

Half an hour out of Paris I turned off the autoroute and made a sweep south of the city, past Versailles. I kept off the marked routes, which meant I lost myself a couple of times. It also meant that if they had cars looking out for me in St-Germain-en-Laye and the slip roads near Vaucresson, or waiting at Porte d'Auteuil or Porte St-Cloud, I would miss trouble.

I pulled into the side of the road, with a sight of the new buildings at Rungis, sheltering the little Renault 5 behind one of those grey square structures that Electricité de France puts up, like a cement memorial outside every village. I stopped because a lot of thoughts kept pushing forward and the entry to Paris is no time to be driving on automatic pilot. Also I had to make certain there was no tail.

Twenty-eight.

When I was twenty-three, twenty-four, twenty-five, I was certain.

I would go through the routines—if it was in a car—holding back at traffic lights, indicating right and turning left, U-turn in front of oncoming truck, the usual. I would be certain. No tail.

But I'm wiser, I'm twenty-eight. I know there's always another way.

The loner is easy to mark. He has to stay attached. If you've any doubts, get a wedge of traffic between yourselves, hold back in a side turning and come up suddenly on him from behind. Look in his face as you reappear in his rear view mirror. Only a very old dog won't let relief flood his eyes.

The team is a nuisance because it takes longer.

But it's the latecomers you're not prepared for, latecomers because they know your route up to a certain point. After you've driven an hour and a half it's hard not to stop confidence taking over. You're approaching Paris, the traffic is thickening. Your attention focuses on driving problems. You don't pick out the dark green family saloon among the clutter.

So stop.

I checked the traffic that passed the EDF substation. Champigneulles delivery truck, yellow PTT van, commercials in their Simcas and Opels and Amis, bus taking a roadgang somewhere.

I'd rented from Avis.

I could have tried harder.

I could have borrowed a car from J. Old times sake. No recriminations. Maybe dinner, in a little while. But it had been Avis and I'd had no time to arrange anything but my real driving permit, real *carte de séjour*, and that's how Crevecoeur had put a finger on me. Others could too.

There could be someone checking car numbers at the end of the autoroute. Or worse, there could be a bug in the car. They'd had time enough. I might be driving round screaming "Here comes Cody" to a following car or a nerve centre in Paris.

Hopeless. Turn in the car.

Those were technical considerations. There was a lot else to evaluate in what Crevecoeur had told me. He'd gone by the morning, my account settled. There was no note, no future rdv. There was no need.

I sat. The traffic went past and the names moved round my brain: Dee, Crevecoeur, Ladouceur, Agate, Pasquier.

Pasquier: out of four and a half thousand journalists in Paris, he was the one with the hot line to Ladouceur's story. Why him?

Ladouceur: someone I'd never encountered but he was growing very real in my mind: brilliant, enthusiastic, compassionate, radical. A good man? His wife's judgement.

Dee: on edge, concealing, concealing.

Then there were the people Agate said had flown into Paris: Duraine and McKosker. I knew them, God how I knew them. I had first run into Duraine in Berlin, where he was Station Head for the Agency. And then in Turkey they had both tricked me into doing a dirty little job for the Agency. McKosker was tough, a cheat, a veteran from half the unhappy countries of the world. Duraine was devious, with eyes like a lizard, and he'd rather twist you round his finger than give you something straight. Duraine would relish Cold War games. He frightened me as much as the man with the rifle among the long loaves.

I sat, images and names crowding my brain, swamping me with deceit and trickery. It felt too much.

I locked the car and went into a café down the road and got a couple of *jetons* for the telephone. There were the usual three men in blue overalls at the bar and a fat woman wiping glasses, bored eye on the television in the corner.

There was a special news broadcast. The President was holding a cabinet meeting in Dijon, showing he was involved in important affairs of State even while electioneering, and that he was not remote from the regions.

The TV showed black Peugeot 604s arriving outside the Préfecture in Dijon, Ministers with attaché cases looking purposeful for the camera before hurrying inside. Which was Crevecoeur's secret agent? What did it matter. In two hours there'd be more pictures of them leaving, looking purposeful. The communiqué would announce they had discussed new initiatives on inflation and unemployment. That would mean they had discussed election prospects. The President was trailing eight points in the opinion polls.

It was a pointless exercise, the government leaning on ORTF for propaganda. Pointless because the deluge had already started, in that day's *Courrier,* and by the evening French political allegiances would be overturned.

My first phone call was Avis, regrets, the car had been stolen, I would mail the key.

Second call to the local police, a stolen car was abandoned, EDF substation, entrance to village. And who's reporting this, madame?

I replaced the receiver.

They could sort it out between them. If the local police were ambitious, they might even discover Crevecoeur's prints.

I waited nearly two hours for a bus. I wasn't bored. I had the *Courrier* to read.

The scandal of the secret project.

86

Pasquier had gone to town in a way no American or British paper does any more.

"Evidence has reached this reporter," he thundered, "of a scandalous nature. There are reports that nobody in authority, at the Institut 21, in the government, even the President himself, has been able to deny. Only the *Courrier,* in an exclusive article, exposes what Jean-Louis Ladouceur has really been up to in his lavishly appointed ivory tower in Paris.

"He has been working for the Soviet Union.

"For the past three months Ladouceur has been deeply involved in a *hush-hush* project commissioned by the government of the USSR, for the most gigantic undertaking in the history of mankind. It is nothing less than the transformation of 100,000 square kilometres of Russian semi-desert to productive farmland and the bringing of new industries on a vast scale to this new economic wonderland.

"The scheme is gigantic in scope, in money terms, in materials involved and in the time scale. It is to last for six decades.

"Ladouceur has drawn up a *blueprint* to reverse the flow of three mighty rivers (the Ob, the Yenisei and the Irtysh) that flow through Siberia and empty uselessly into the Arctic Ocean. Dams and walls will be constructed at the mouths of these rivers, creating an artificial freshwater sea larger than England, raising the whole water-table in the bleak, uninhabited, inhospitable region.

"Then, in this daring scheme, by means of giant aqueducts and the Turgay Canal, this water will be returned south to irrigate vast areas of the Caspian desert and the Volga basin, to bring life back to the sinking Caspian Sea itself, to provide water to quench the mighty thirst of Soviet heavy industry (including the armaments industry) in an area stretching as far west as Sevastopol.

"The amount of earth to be moved is estimated as 16,000,000,000 cubic metres—equal to constructing one hundred Panama Canals. The cost: a staggering 250 billion US dollars, and that is just for the initial stages. Nobody has been able to put a price tag on the finished scheme. But this is not wild science fiction. This is fact. Ladouceur's project is rolling now.

"What is scandalous is that this scheme, which will make the Soviet Union the most economically powerful nation on earth, is being drawn up by a French scientist, in the French Institut 21, supported by French taxpayers.

"But had anybody ever asked us French our opinion?

"Has anybody ever asked you what you think about a Frenchman working to promote the power and glory of communist Russia?

"Where is this *globe-trotter* now, this brilliant Ladouceur? Why has he vanished? What harm is he doing to France while you read this? Why is he not working for the economic betterment of France, of you and your children?

"We the French demand answers."

Poor French people: they deserved better than the answers they got.

Paris was brooding under heavy clouds and a north-east wind and even the German tourists weren't smiling. No one was smiling.

Le Courrier publishes just before midnight and if you are so inclined you can buy an early edition on your way home to bed. For once they published early, to catch the crowds after work and going out for the evening.

I had gone back to the Hotel Moderne. I had been explicit that no one should enter the room, not even the maid. I said my lungs were dust-reactive and to make the bed or sweep the carpet would disturb the dust and I would be unable to breathe without acute discomfort. I think if I'd had luggage, the man would have assumed I was concealing something valuable or dangerous, but I'd brought nothing.

No one had been in my room. I'd done the usual with a fragment of tissue in the door hinge and a hair at the edge of a drawer. If anybody had discovered where I was staying, they would, as routine, have searched the room, or they'd be waiting inside. It was still secure.

It was after six when I went out. Cold but no fresh snow. I was glad of the dark: it shadowed the dirt that settles on left-over snow in cities.

I walked to the boul Mich and it is the only time I have seen it in my life: people actually lining up to buy newspapers, standing in knots on street corners, reading, questioning, trying to take in the importance of the story.

Only Pasquier had it. The *Courrier's* headline screamed:

There will be no more champagne!!

When the business was long over and I could see the whole of it in perspective, I thought about it once. It almost made me smile. It was a caricature of being French. The story was about the end of civilization as France knew it and they summed it up: no more champagne.

Pasquier's style had become ever more shrill. He had either been fed more exciting titbits from his unnamed source or had been talking to someone qualified to interpret the effects of Ladouceur's river reversal scheme.

The effects on the climate of France would be cataclysmic.

I recalled Pasquier's words at Les Trois Marias: "If it doesn't rain in Normandy, no grass, no cows, no camembert. That's how a journalist vulgarizes climatology and geo-economics."

The point, beneath the hysteria, was stark: by reversing the rivers the whole ecological balance of the land mass from the Arctic Ocean to the Caspian and Black Seas would be profoundly affected. If the intention were to bring these cold waters through the Ural Mountains, then a huge cold damp mass would be created in European Russia. Its effects on temperature, rainfall, wind and other climatic factors were frightening. Not just Russia but the whole of northern Europe would be affected. It was only south of the Alps and the Massif Central that the Mediterranean Sea would have a countering influence. For over half of France it would be the equivalent of shifting the country two hundred kilometres further north. Hence: no more champagne.

Other points he made: The fruit orchards of Normandy, Brittany, Alsace and the Loire were threatened. New cereal and salad crops would be needed. All buildings would require extra insulation. There would be extra expenditure on clothes, bedding and fuel. There would be dire economic problems for energy-poor France. More French would holiday abroad; fewer foreign tourists would visit the country, leading to serious financial troubles for the hotel, catering and wine industries, and the country's international payments. The franc would sink in value, the cost of living would soar, every family in the land would be poorer.

Pasquier could never have worked it all out. Who was prompting him and why?

I had intended to go and see Dolbiac. Instead, I ate at a small Vietnamese restaurant and concentrated on the Pasquier scoop. I was puzzled, worried, frightened; and not just about a cold Europe.

I could not see the next moves in Crevecoeur's Cold War games.

France was being destabilized.

I had never lived in a country, seen it actually tearing itself apart. I cursed Duraine, McKosker and everyone in the Agency whose name I knew.

It came with the speed of a blizzard. There were arguments on street corners that evening and I witnessed a fight through a café window. Before the night was over it was much worse.

11

The light went out.

There was no warning.

I was over the foot of the bed, prone on the floor, in three seconds. If they were coming for me a third time, bed would be the first place they'd look. But they might not look, they might simply shoot. Similarly, I didn't want to be upright anywhere in the bedroom because they might shoot out the lock before storming in: a standing body presents a much greater target than a prone one.

I breathed out shallowly, through my mouth, shivering. How had they found me?

Half a minute, maybe more, passed and I thought: They're waiting till I come to check the light switch by the door. When they hear the click of the switch, they'll know my body position. So I waited, not moving.

I had no gun. I would never carry a gun of my own because it grows familiar. Even a person who maintains that it is only for show, to impress, ends by using it. The process is inevitable: what is a gun for if not to be used? The argument has no answer. You can see the same thought process in generals: what are nuclear weapons for if we can't use them? For three decades the generals have grown accustomed to nuclear weapons—nukes, a pet name even—and they're hungry to try, just this once. The only reason they haven't is that the presidents and prime ministers, the ones who hold the keys to the locks, change every four or five years; they never have the time to grow familiar with the doomsday machine they control.

But I wanted a gun now. Because if they didn't come in for me, I was going to have to go out for them.

There was a noise from the corridor, footsteps, knocking on

the door next to mine, voices. Someone called out, *"C'est putain"*, but not referring to a hotel guest. The knock came on my door. I knew what I had to do.

"What is it?"

And then I was rolling to one side. They might pinpoint my position even through the closed door: the wood wasn't thick.

"Do you have electricity?"

"No."

"It is the whole building. I think the power has been cut."

Footsteps receded into silence.

I went to the window, parted the curtain a fraction. There were no lights in neighbouring buildings and even at 1 am there should be some. From my position there was a view of three street lamps and they gave no light.

It wasn't just the hotel. It was affecting Paris itself.

By the morning, electricity was restored. The radio in the café where I had breakfast said it was a lightning strike by the electricity supply workers. They were protesting because of the Russian river reversal scheme. They were demanding action, a meeting with someone, they weren't certain who. The protest was directionless, like the aimless arguments at my bar. They ought to do something, they ought to stop this happening, they ought to take action to save France.

Who should act?

Well, the government, the President. That's what he's there for. To do something.

What can he do?

He can protest to the bloody Russians, he can stop Ladouceur working to destroy us all.

The radio was carrying reports of walk-outs at factories throughout the country: a textile plant at Roubaix, Michelin at Clermont-Ferrand, Aerospatiale at Toulouse, Air Inter. The 8.30 Air France flight to Moscow had been cancelled when the crew refused to cross a picket line at Charles de Gaulle airport.

To bring down a government, to destabilize the whole fabric of a country, requires pressure over a prolonged period. Witness the Agency's long drawn out action against Allende. But with a limited goal, the effects can be seen very soon.

I didn't know whether there were *agents provocateurs* or whether it was spontaneous. But it started, it grew, and it spread.

There were people running past the window of the café I was

in. Two men went to the door to peer out, and then they were running the same way. I paid for the coffee and croissant and joined them.

I walked up a block to where a small crowd had gathered. They were shouting, but it was angry and ragged rather than a disciplined chant and I couldn't make out the words. The focus of emotion was a small shop which had been empty and was now taken over by the Communist Party for a local office during the election period.

After the Communist—Socialist split, after the on—off marriage of convenience, the two parties had finally come together again for the presidential election. It wasn't a principled alliance, it was an expedient like all political alliances. They realized that apart they would fail; together they would succeed. And so this office fascia carried a red banner exhorting the workers to support the presidential candidate of the United Left.

There were fists beating on the door.

I was still fifty metres away when a man thrust a handbill at me, gestured at the Communist office and shouted, *"Les salauds."* He'd gone, another handbill ready to thrust at someone else.

Already the Reds serve Moscow!!

The headline was a shriek, the message just as shrill: France was threatened by a Soviet scheme, devised by a traitorous Frenchman. Why weren't the communists protesting? Because they were the lackeys of the Kremlin, the enemies of France.

As I left I heard the first stone.

There were two policemen watching. What could they do against two hundred?

There were meetings all over that morning. In the afternoon I saw two separate marches. The government was caught unaware by the speed of the protests, or the efficiency of the protest organization, and was uncertain what to do. The mood of the crowds was volatile in the extreme. One moment it was the government's fault: why was Giscard not doing anything to save France from destruction by the Soviet Union? Then someone would cry out: it was a communist plot and why wasn't the PCF saying anything? Because their hearts belonged in Moscow, not here.

There were fights. Nothing was certain.

I was in a crowd at the Rond-Point on the Champs-Elysées when chance and irrationality settled the matter in the public mind. It began to snow again.

As the first big flakes fell, a man hauled himself half-way up a lamp-post. He flung an arm out to the north-east, where the clouds hung blackest.

"It's begun already! It'll be winter for ever in France unless we stop the Reds!"

There was no television crew present but a similar incident was shown on TV news that evening. A man bellowed at camera: "We'll be living in Moscow not Paris if the communists have their way. We'll have eight months winter. We'll be begging the Russians for food."

It could have been the same man. He had an identical voice, rough with black tobacco and red wine and bawling at street meetings.

It had taken twenty-four hours to become fixed in the public consciousness: a radical marxist was scheming to serve Russia at the expense of France, and if the communists weren't stopped it would be the death of the country.

And this destabilization, this covert operation, is what Agate had tried to warn me of?

Newspapers became an addiction. In the afternoon I plunged into the grey world of *Le Monde*. President Giscard had returned with some speed to Paris and held an emergency cabinet meeting at the Elysée Palace. The agenda had only one item. Afterwards, the Minister for Information held a conference for press and television and announced the government's response to events.

1. Firm action would be taken to maintain law and order. All leave in the Gendarmerie, Gardes Mobiles and CRS had been cancelled. Rioting would not be tolerated and protest meetings in the cities would require the permission of the Prefect.

2. Energetic measures would be taken to ascertain the whereabouts of Monsieur Ladouceur. Border posts and airports were put on full alert.

3. A message had already been sent to the Soviet government requesting information on the assistance Monsieur Ladouceur was affording.

4. A committee of distinguished scientists was being appointed to evaluate what effects a river reversal scheme in the Soviet Union would have on French climatic conditions.

It was good soothing stuff.

It had no effect on public opinion. A communist election rally in Besançon was broken up and the early evening TV news reported: *A Besançon, un mort, dix-sept blessés.*

He answered my knock and I noticed the change at once. There are little things: the curve of lips, the light in the eyes, the hand that lingers as it passes you into the room. The signs were missing, all missing.

I didn't ask. I tried not to show I'd noticed.

The room was in darkness except for the lamp angled up to throw its beam on the attic-pitched ceiling. Dolbiac went back to a chair, closed his eyes. I sat on the floor, said nothing.

I didn't know where Dolbiac had got the record that was playing. He didn't like Mozart, didn't dispute the genius, simply didn't like the music. It was a string quartet, full of melancholy. Its mood affected me.

There was silence when the record player clicked and was still.

"Mozart," Dolbiac said it as if he didn't have to say any more. His eyes stayed shut. And then, "Four instruments going round and round, searching for a tiny beauty."

I heard the wind worrying at the wooden frame of the window.

"Four weak voices and even together they don't add up to the power or the breadth or the colour of a single piano."

It was, I suppose, a natural viewpoint for him; but narrow.

"Where did you get the record?"

There was a pause. Normally we spoke French but when he replied it was in English: "A friend."

"A friend?"

I didn't understand. And then I did. To say it in French would mean giving away the sex of the friend.

And so I knew, inside myself. In trying to conceal, he'd made it clear. I had been growing to expect it, the idea of someone else in his life, because it was the explanation for the change in him: the gaiety and wit and spontaneity I had loved that had vanished, the eyes that had once pierced right inside me that now turned aside.

I wondered who she was. Was it pride I didn't ask?

But there was a pride in him too: something he had found out about me which he didn't mention. There was a long silence while he didn't tell me.

We sat and the illumination from the single light source made striking pools of brightness and eerie shadows, contrasty as Hitchcock, lighting a cheek, a nose, hiding the expression in the deeps of the eyes.

In the room the silence was no longer the easy acceptance of friendship. It could have been the minor key of the Mozart, sad notes of violas and cello. But I thought, suddenly, this was the end, the last time.

If only he'd told me.

"Canuck."

He opened his eyes. I could see nothing there.

We ate a little, opened a bottle of Beaune, didn't finish it. There was some talk. But he didn't ask where I'd been for two nights, didn't say the important thing. Pride?

We went to bed, naked under the covers, the wind trying to get at us through the shutters. We made love. No longer the fierceness of possession in him. It was slow, but the slowness was not sweetness or consideration; it was spacing out because inside was the haunting thought: was this the last time?

He put his hand behind and rolled me over so that we lay side by side, faces a handspan apart, eyes searching.

We all search. The truth we find never lasts.

When the precipice came there was the shudder, and the rattle of the wind in the windowframe seemed part of it. I felt his warmth and my heartbeats. I touched his forehead and it seemed like dew.

Canuck, I'm sorry.

If only I'd stayed away that night.

12

They took me at dawn.

I awoke, grey light filtering through shutters. The weight of the last days had dragged me down to a level of sleep I hardly ever reach. I must have broken through to consciousness during one of those periods of rapid eye-movements when we dream. I struggled with the alien image in my mind; black girl, naked, tattoos of needle marks over her arms and legs and breasts, and I had been bending down to kiss the blood from one of the nipples. The black girl had the face of Dee, with rust markings above the eyes like the Doberman. She was sobbing and I was comforting her with caresses, each stroke sinking lower.

I'm not normally attracted to other women but the dream had been powerful enough to leave me confused.

I reached out but there was only the hollow where Dolbiac had been. It was still warm from his body and I wished he was there because I needed the reassurance of feeling the rough hairs across his shoulders to block out the persisting memory of running fingers over her belly.

It wasn't a struggle against forbidden fruit. My nature wanted to reassert itself.

I heard the voices but not what they were saying until there was the sound of a smash from Dolbiac's studio/living room and louder, *"Putaing."*

It was the accent from down in the Midi, from round Toulon and Marseille, and I was coming up rapidly while I was working this out when the door to the bedroom opened and three of them came in. The centre light turned on and I saw three Browning automatics. It's a gun the French police favour, when they don't use machine pistols.

One of the faces had a familiarity but there was no time to work it out.

I wasn't certain who the people I'd glimpsed in street shadows recently had been, but I was certain what these were not. The French police forces, in their variety, use some strange types but they exhibit one common characteristic: when they break open a room their eyes are everywhere, hungry for hidden trouble, exits, traps, other guns. These were not police: they looked only at me.

Three strides and one of them ripped back the sheet and they got that stupid grin on their faces and another said, *"J'ai une pine d'ours, tu sais,"* and guffawed.

The human brain works at two levels. On the top of the heap was the query: What had happened to Dolbiac? Underneath was the idea I didn't want to examine in full light: rape; three men staring, the reference to having a bear's prick. One man had red weals on his cheek and my conscious mind said Dolbiac, and then the lower level started to work so that when I moved—it could have been after three seconds—I had already checked out courses of action.

But I made the wrong assumption: Corsicans or *pieds noirs* with an interest in robbery or rape.

In the fragment of time before I committed myself I knew it depended on whether they were ordinarily stupid or very stupid. If they were very stupid nothing I would say would get through to their brains and I would run into hot metal travelling at 1500 fps.

I had to shout because their attention was distracted by my naked body.

"Your guns are no good. You're finished if you shoot."

It pulled their faces up and I could make out the first wrinkles of confusion. Simple words are best.

"You can't use a gun. Don't shoot. The neighbours will hear. You'll have the whole building up here with the noise."

Lie. But had they the time or the intelligence to check? Because of the piano, Dolbiac had had to pay for sound insulation, walls, ceiling, under the carpet. You could play the 1812, complete with cannons, and no one would hear. But it worried them.

I saw the one nearest the door slacken his jaw and drop his eyes to the Browning in his hand.

The doubt had been set up and it had to be now before they grew accustomed to the idea that guns were out and it was back to unarmed stuff.

I was grateful to the one who'd pulled back the sheet. My legs were free and I swung them over to the floor and set out for the window.

Nobody fired.

Dolbiac's apartment was at the top of an old building, twenty-five metres from the edge of the mansard roof to the courtyard and the downpipe from the gutter hardly took the rainwater, let alone the weight of a human body. But I had to separate them.

The one who'd pulled the sheet moved first, jumping on the bed and across and down on the window side, left arm reaching for me and I swung round on the ball of my foot and accepted the outstretched hand and helped him on his way, heading for the wall. He must have cried out as his skull connected but my brain was too occupied to accept the sound.

The momentum I'd gained by pulling him started me back across the floor towards the other two, still by the door but starting to move.

I was already set on going for the one on the left because he was further away from the hinge side of the door and I'd have more room to swing him; in fact I aimed to hit the wall to his side so that I could use the impact to change direction. It would be a hand throw, but swivelling my hip so that I used his forward motion to put him over in the path of the other.

I didn't decide consciously, it was reaction. The thing about judo and savate is by the time you're proficient enough to use your hands and feet in this kind of situation, the moves come without much involvement from the conscious brain. Analogy with walking: you don't have to issue instructions to pelvis and leg muscles and knee joint for each step. The brain had said divide them and use one to block the other and then make for the next room and check Dolbiac and get the door to the stairs open, and the body was supplying the necessary moves according to behaviour patterns I had rehearsed in non-lethal situations.

And then I stopped dead.

I stopped because of my fundamental error.

I'd assumed they had come for basic power gratification—sex and money—and perhaps the sexual assumption had been implanted by the shadows the dream had left behind in my brain.

I halted when my path diagonally across the open door brought the studio/living room within my field of vision. There were two more. One in a white coat had his arms folded and his head angled towards the bedroom with its sudden eruption of violent noise. The other stood behind Dolbiac, who'd flung on a bathrobe to answer the door, and held a knife to his neck, just below the right ear. The point of the knife rested on the skin and I could even see the slight depression it made.

The skin there is no more than a millimetre thick. So thin to hold in the life of a man.

They had come for another purpose and I hadn't connected them with Ladouceur. If only Dolbiac hadn't hidden it from me.

The man in the white coat kept his arms folded but made a gesture with a hand.

"It would be better if you got dressed."

The accent told me nothing, or too much. It was American, but sounded like a Swede who had lived there. No help.

I pushed slowly past the two thugs into the living room. Dolbiac stood stiff and awkward and still.

"Close enough," the man in the white coat said.

There was no sensible move I could make. A knife is very quiet, quick too when it's zero distance from the target. I could think of no questions I would be given answers to.

"Your clothes."

I got dressed in the bedroom, the two apes watching but no longer grinning, the one with the sore head gone to look for a bottle. Dolbiac kept mute. He knew this affair was to do with me; I assumed they'd said as much when they came through the front door.

I had one tiny consoling thought. Crevecoeur said they would want me alive now and he was being proved correct.

The one in the white coat told me to push my sleeve up. He was scrupulous with the cotton wool and ether and I watched the needle slip in.

It was quick.

I had time to wonder where they would take me as they moved to Dolbiac. I watched the needle go into his arm and he glared at me.

"Co, for God's sake."

His face was bewildered and outraged.

Then he made his move and I should have cried out to him: *Canuck, don't be a hero.* But the drug was already touching my brain. I saw his movement and the flashing answer from the man next to him. But my brain refused to accept what I saw. It was a mercy then, hell later.

It was at this precise moment I noticed something about the perspective of the walls I'd never taken in before.

Strange of Canuck. He'd got Salvador Dali to do the interior décor, distorting the right angles and undulating the flat surfaces. When had Canuck got Dali in? How could he afford him? I looked at the ceiling: it was waving like seaweed. Hi, ceiling. And wow, the bed. Salvador Dali had stretched the bed to infinity. Well, of course I'd heard stories about Sally. And the headboard was melting like warm chocolate. Trust good old Sal.

Out.

I was a child again.

The difference between sleep and unconsciousness is that during sleep three senses are still active: feel, smell, hearing. They continue to send signals to the brain to warn of any potential danger.

Whereas while you're unconscious, the body is annihilated.

I had been annihilated, and came alive in a series of bumps on an upward graph curve, memories, a jumble of brief messages from my awakening senses, with troughs of nothing in between, but rising steadily up to the light where my brain could begin to take grip.

Why was I a child? There was an image in my mind, eight in the evening, my father coming into my bedroom. I could feel the smoothness of the pillow on my cheek. My father's face was drained by the day, haunted by the pain and sufferings of others. And even if the sufferings were imaginary, they were real.

Irrelevancies first.

They must have used a stretcher to get me downstairs. Plausible if they met a neighbour.

Only *me* considered in my struggling mind.

Then I thought of Dolbiac. The memory had the force of an axe. I pushed it away; I wasn't strong enough yet.

Again, why was I a child? The feeling of the pillow on my cheek and next the smell, the smell my father carried in from the surgery. My father had been a doctor. The smell was registering, smell of antiseptics and medicaments, taking me back to childhood.

Getting much better. I was beginning to reason.

There was sudden centrifugal force and I gripped with my hands to steady my body. I opened my eyes: underwater gloom and rotating of a square of dim illumination.

I closed my eyes, reopened, moved my head and made the rotating square steady. It was dark glass and I got it.

Ambulance.

And that face with the troubling familiarity as they had burst into the bedroom: one of the ambulancemen who'd picked Agate up in the street.

I felt a flood of emotion. I didn't want to end up in hospital with the drip bottle of chloral hydrate.

"You can't move." It was the man in the white coat, behind my head. He was out of vision but the voice was distinctive. "You are strapped so you don't roll out when we corner."

Straps bit across my chest, arms, and just above the knees. I could raise and move my head. I looked and there was no other stretcher.

So then I had to ask: "Where's Dolbiac?"

The man replied: "We left him. We laid him by the door to the concierge's apartment. She'll get him to a doctor."

"God, why did you do it?"

I don't know whether there was regret on his face. There was none in his voice. "It was his fault. He should not have moved."

I remembered with vivid clarity. Before the drug took effect, Dolbiac had made a move to grab the provençale pot, some notion of a weapon, and the knife had come down like a guillotine.

I tried to blank the memory. I tried to recall the Dali-esque fantasies I'd had, which had blotted out reality.

Reality came back at me. The knife had met Dolbiac's hand and severed the index finger at the lower joint. The first finger on his right hand. There are no four-fingered pianists. I heard his scream now; I had censored it then. He would have felt pain, before the drug released him. When he awoke he'd know pain again, and pain for the rest of his life, the pain of loss, an artist destroyed.

"Why? Why?"

"He made a mistake. Learn from his mistake."

I had other questions but I didn't think there were any answers: who the man was, why I had been taken, where Ladouceur was, what my destination was, all that.

There was no way of computing how long I'd been under. I concentrated on the speed and progress of the ambulance, and decided we'd left Paris. There were none of the checks that city traffic imposes.

"How did you know to come to Dolbiac's apartment?"

There was a silence and I thought I wasn't going to get an answer.

"Because of his connection with you."

"Connection?"

"He went to your apartment."

Canuck, you should have told me last night. We would have been out of your apartment so fast, with at least a chance.

In my building he would have run into Madame Boyer and she might well have prevented him going up. She'd take pleasure in saying I'd spent the last two nights out, and so he'd been cold with me. Of course they were watching and followed.

"But..."

"No more questions."

The ambulance wasn't using its alarm, no emergency, just transferring a patient. I could be heading anywhere. The man in the white coat appeared at my side, steadying himself with one hand on the roof. The other hand held the hypodermic. Needle-time again. Why?

He squatted beside me. I concentrated on his face instead of watching the needle go in, but there was nothing in his eyes. He was experienced with a hypodermic, which was a small comfort, showed some professional knowledge if not ethics. He'd be aware of dangers. You can't keep pumping the stuff in. The body's not built like that.

Old movies used to have ripple-dissolves to signal a flashback. The world was already losing its structure at the edges of my vision and I was back in the Salvador Dali fantasy with the knife flashing and the echo of the cry. If I built up anger thinking about Dolbiac and raised my blood pressure and concentrated my will, I might delay the darkness for half a minute, but it was inevitable.

At first the sound was part of the nightmare. Grumble over to the left, growing louder, roaring towards me. I felt no panic.

Louder, louder. The ambulance braked to a halt.

It thundered overhead while my brain made the supreme leap. Jet plane. Airport.

13

It was Day Four in the white cube.

It was my best reckoning though I couldn't be positive. They'd taken away my watch. Without that reference we judge time by what we see around us and what we feel within. But my environment was totally controlled so I had only my internal body clocks to guide me.

I am no chronobiological expert but I am fully aware that the human body is built not just from muscle and bone but from time as well. I strived for total recall of everything I had learned about the behaviour of the body under artificial stress conditions.

It seemed I was in a hospital room, or possibly a medical unit within some penal institution. The room was in fact three times as long as it was high but I thought of it as a cube. I had a sense of being trapped in some piece of functional art that should be exhibited at the Guggenheim with a title card: "The Cube Root of 20th-century Man".

My cube was all-over white, not for reasons of hospital hygiene but because white is pitiless.

A raised platform against one wall held a foam rubber mattress, a pillow, a white coverlet. The floor was some rubberised composition. A cubicle held a shower, toilet and basin. There was a drinking cup of crushable plastic. The soap had no marking on it. An anonymous tube held toothpaste; there was no toothbrush. When I had found out how to communicate, I'd asked for a toothbrush and they had said, No. I asked why and there was no response. I thought about it and decided it was because the plastic handle could be fashioned into a dagger of some kind.

They would not be concerned I would overwhelm them; they were worried I would try to open one of my own veins.

The thought sustained me. I had some value to them, therefore they would be at pains not to destroy me. Knowing that, I had some small lever of power against them.

The ceiling held a ventilation grid, a loudspeaker and a video camera. There was no window. There was a slight lingering smell of *eau de Javel,* the smell you get in that kind of place no matter which country it is.

I had no memory of arriving in the room. I had woken once, briefly, on the plane. My mind had been too confused to note much more than that I was still strapped to the stretcher. The man in the white coat had come, lifted one of my eyelids, looked into my despair. The needle had appeared and reality slipped away.

So I had woken in the room on what I termed Day One. I don't know what they had pushed into me but I felt waves of nausea I had never experienced before. The nausea seemed to start in my toes, sweep through my body and come out of my eyes and mouth and nose all at once. I didn't vomit. The nausea passed and was replaced by fear. I would have welcomed the nausea back again. I was afraid of the anonymity. I was in a world without identity, neither personal identity nor physical identity, without time, without reason, without knowledge of my adversaries, without hope of release or even death. I was afraid because of what I knew they were going to do. They weren't going to be crude; there would be no thumbscrews. They were going to strip me of my personality by destroying reality. They were starting with the physical environment I was held captive in: anonymous, totally controlled, a battery house for one bird. They would progress to me: my past, my relationships, my beliefs would be destroyed; my brain, my emotions, my right to a separate existence would crumble. I would be manipulated by isolation, rewards, punishment, hypnosis, drugs, sense of time. My identity would go. I would be theirs. Whatever they wanted to know they would discover. When I was sucked dry, I would have no further use. I would cease to exist.

Day One had been the worst.

There had been the footsteps.

I had tried the door, pushing with my shoulder because there was no handle on my side. By putting my ear to it I could hear the faint hum of some distant machinery. Then I thought a swing door opened and footsteps grew louder. I began hammering and shouting. I don't know what words.

The footsteps faded.

I had caught a movement above in the corner of my eye. I swung to face the room. The video camera found me and stopped. The lens caught an angle of light and it stared, unblinking.

"You may beat at the door if it helps reduce tension." The voice issued from the loudspeaker. "No one will come."

I had discovered how to communicate. I asked questions and received some responses. Usually there was nothing. It grew unbearable when I asked and received nothing in reply. The sense of being abandoned worsened; so I stopped trying to communicate.

Except that I had asked for the toothbrush and was denied it. And then I yelled at them, "The light's broken."

"The light has not broken. It is time to sleep."

There was total blackness, not even a chink of light under the door.

After an hour or so the light came on again. The voice said: "It is time to wake up."

"But I haven't been to sleep yet. It was only dark for a short time."

"You are wrong, just as you are wrong about other things. The night passed."

Then I'd lain on the bunk and concentrated on what I knew of my body and brain processes. I had wasted time. If I wanted to survive I should have started already.

It had been the very end of the night when they had come to Dolbiac's apartment, 6 am or a little later. I was transported by an ambulance to a functioning airport, not a deserted airstrip. Therefore there would be formalities with Immigration about the transfer of a patient. That was assuming I had been flown across the frontier. The alternative: I hadn't passed through Immigration because it was an internal flight (I would now be somewhere like the Vosges); or a flight plan had been filed for a stage to, say, Mulhouse-Basle airport and the plane had simply dipped down and continued east. From my brief interlude of semi-lucidity I knew the jet I'd been in was not a small executive craft. Therefore the speed could be taken as approximately 850-900 kph.

Conclusions: I was taken from the apartment at 6.15. Transport to the airport outside Paris, formalities, transfer to waiting plane—one and a half hours. Flight time: minimum of one hour (anything else would have made ambulance transport more convenient), maximum of three and a half hours (I didn't think it could be further east than Moscow). Transfer to the institution: under an hour. Regaining consciousness: unknown, but unlikely to be more than thirty minutes.

By my reckoning, I surfaced at no later than midday and very likely earlier.

I had examined my cell, beaten on the door, questioned the unseen voice, lain down, fought to regain control of my will. Two men in orderly's clothing had brought a stew of beef and carrots, bread, an apple. I had eaten under the eye of the video camera, and the tray had been removed. That had been the only food during what they had been pleased to call a day. The light had been switched off by my estimate somewhere during the timespan 4 to 6 p.m.

I hadn't slept. The light had come on and I was told it was a new day.

A tray had been brought with bread, jam and coffee. I was not hungry. My stomach was still digesting the previous meal. Since the liquid stew had not been physically processed as far as requiring me to urinate, I thought no more than an hour had elapsed.

They were trying to tell me it was my second day of captivity. My body function and brain told me; it might still be no later than 6 p.m. on Day One.

The light stayed on and nothing happened.

I had told the video camera I had a headache. I was brought two aspirins. I went into the ablution cubicle, to the only place the camera could not see, and concealed the aspirins behind the toilet. Later I told the camera the headache had not passed. Now I had four aspirins hidden. I planned to keep trying for aspirins. It depended how long I was held, but there could come a situation where I wanted to close the shutters on my life; if I amassed enough aspirin there was the possibility I could swallow a final dose without vomiting.

It was a negative thought, the only one I allowed. I shut it off from further consideration.

We eat, digest, use energy, rest and sleep in a rhythmic way. In this century, with the urban breakdown of the natural relationship between night/rest and day/activity, this rhythm is disturbed. But it is not broken. We have twenty thousand, perhaps thirty thousand, generations of humans behind us and the natural clocks are implanted deep in our make-up. They cannot be tampered with in a short period, provided we guard against it.

We think we respond only to night and day, the rhythm of waking, working during the light, sleeping during the dark. But we're affected by the rhythms of gravity, the pull of the moon and tides, electromagnetic fields, air pressures, sound. Divorced from the discipline of night/day, our bodies adapt to a period that is neither a solar day of exactly 24 hours nor a lunar day of 24-8 hours. We each develop our own circadian rhythm, somewhere about a solar day in length, but varying between 23 and 26 hours according to the individual. Energy, emotions, hunger, tiredness flow in a constant pattern.

All this I know because at Langley they'd said: "Never believe what they tell you, believe what your body tells you."

I disregarded their artificial day/night. I listened to my body clocks, my stomach, my bodily functions, the alertness of my brain and senses. I needed to establish my own rhythm, to keep control over my life.

I judged it to be late evening on Day One and I spoke to the camera.

"I'm hungry."

"It is not lunch time yet."

I knew it wasn't even the second day, but I kept the knowledge to myself. It could be important at a later stage that they should believe I was disoriented and my time-structure destroyed; whereas it would be intact. Another gramme of power over them.

Later a tray had been brought in. I ate. The tray was taken away.

I had lain down and shut my eyes against the light.

The voice: "It is not night yet."

"I'm tired."

Then the noises began. They came from the speaker, soft at first, insinuating into my brain, growing louder. There were boots, military boots, marching across a parade ground. They grew nearer, suddenly very loud, and there was no escape, even with my hands over my ears. At a formless cry of command, the boots crashed to a halt. Again a cry with no discernible words and I heard a dozen or more rifle bolts slam open and crash shut on rounds of ammunition. The silence drew out. Then the voice without words gave a warning shout, and another, and I was waiting, waiting, waiting for the order to fire and the crack of explosions. Nothing came.

There was sweat on my hands and forehead before I realized what they were doing to me.

I had no watch so I could not measure my pulse rate against time. But I could measure it against my rate of respiration. There were six or seven beats to every breath. I relaxed my body until the rate returned to the normal 4:1. I must not let them get control of my body.

Another tray arrived, so soon after the previous one.

It was the lowpoint of my circadian rhythm when the light went out. My energy, my emotions, my optimism were at the bottom of their curve. I slept and when I awoke it was by my reckoning Day Two, though they were trying to persuade me it was the third day.

On Day Two the pattern had repeated itself. Pressure was applied to convince me that life was passing at twice the speed it was. Trays appeared and were removed, lights were switched on and off. I was kept deprived of human company, the orderlies not speaking and departing within fifteen seconds. I did running and breathing exercises. I decided against trying for more aspirins: suicide would not be my way out.

I determined to live.

I determined to live because suddenly it seemed important, and for more than personal considerations. From my limited time with the Agency I know to be true what everyone suspects: that the idea of a super-agent, a James Bond, saving the world is a puff of imagination. Most never encounter resurgent Nazis creeping out of the jungle nor get to foil terrorists with a nuclear device on board Carter's Air Force One. But this was real: the plan to destabilize France. I had tripped over one of those Cold War manoeuvres that is like an iceberg: I couldn't see the eight-ninths that was below the surface but I would find out, I would escape with the knowledge.

They used the abortive execution technique on me again. But this time the loudspeaker didn't relay boots and rifles, the order to fire never coming. It was a man running across country, his shoes slipping on stones in his panic; his breathing was in gasps and he gave desperate sobs. Behind him started up the sound of pursuing dogs, excited yelps in the distance, then baying, growing closer. There was the clatter of a helicopter and wordless orders through a loudhailer. The footsteps stumbled to a halt and abruptly the dogs were everywhere. I heard the man's breath drawn in for a scream that I waited and waited for. The sound of the dogs continued, worrying at something.

On Day Three, in their false night, there was the sound of a tap dripping. I stumbled to the basin, but it wasn't my tap. It went on, and the sound was gradually processed through an echo chamber. To my brain it should have sounded as if I were going insane. I emptied my mind, forced the sound to retreat.

It was Day Four. We passed through their false seventh day. The play without words was different. I had already been given the execution scene (I knew why the order to fire never came: you don't hear it when it is you who are tied to the post); the futility of escape; the impending madness; now they were implanting the idea of torture. It started with short panting breaths, puzzling at first because they resembled the passionate breathy sounds we make at intimate moments; it turned to crying; then footsteps echoed closer, a lock and bolts were undone, a heavy door opened. There were sharp indrawn sobs, wracking the man's chest. Something like a dentist's drill was started and the hum of it grew louder. The screaming began, high pitched like a girl, surging, then a crescendo. When the screaming stopped, the hum of the machinery was still there; the echo of the scream was inside my skull.

I was pleased. My heart to breathing ratio was steady at 4:1.

In their false night I had time to think without the gaze of the spying camera. Why were they speeding the days so much? They needed to get inside my brain to prise out what I knew about Ladouceur's disappearance; was it the closeness of the election forcing the pace? If so, they'd need to make their move soon.

I was right.

It was on Day Four (during their eighth false day) that I was taken out of the white cube.

During Counter Interrogation Techniques the instructor at the place near Langley had said: "If you're feeling brave, make one abrupt massive jerk with the whole of your upper body. Provided the needle is close to the bone you have a good chance of snapping it off. Oh, it hurts like..." He had broken off, not because I was a woman. He could think of no comparison for the pain.

What they hadn't said during CIT was that it only made sense to break off the needle in your arm if it were the only one available. If you're in a hospital or the Lubianka complex, the pain will achieve nothing. They'll simply fetch a new hypodermic. They might even leave the broken needle in your arm as additional stimulus.

108

There was a tiny consolation: I was certain I wasn't in the Lubianka. This building was modern, seemed only just completed. There were none of the scuffs you find at foot height in institutional buildings.

I didn't resist.

A man I hadn't seen before put the needle in. Two orderlies stood behind. I was seated in a padded plastic chair. I was facing a wall of glowing opaque glass; it was perhaps five metres long and three metres high and filled my field of vision with bright white light. There were three video cameras and my interrogator would be watching on monitors in another room. No possibility of human contact.

"Do you know where you are?"

The voice was aloof. It came from no particular point; they would be using a multi-speaker system. It fitted the pattern. There are only three basic interrogation techniques: threatening, friendly, omniscient. He was playing God, I was an insignificant speck of life with a few tawdry secrets to confess.

"No."

The interrogator continued: "You are being held in an institution for the criminally insane. You have been kept in solitary confinement for well over a week for your own benefit, so that you have time to reflect. There are some questions you must answer and if you behave satisfactorily you will be free to go."

There was one definite lie there, almost certainly two. I would never be free to go.

"If that is understood," the interrogator said, "we'll begin. What is your name?"

My name is Cody. But I wouldn't tell him. I would tell him nothing.

"What is your name?"

He was being ridiculous. What difference could it make. I said: "You know it."

"I want you to tell me your name."

The realization came with a sudden surge. I was more powerful than him. I knew more things than he did. I knew my name and would show him my superiority.

"Cody."

"Is that your real name or your cover?"

"It is mine."

"What is your first name?"

"Call me Cody." We would never be buddies.

"How old are you?"

"I'm twenty-eight."

"Where do you live?"

"Paris."

"Very good, Cody. What street?"

"St-André-des-Arts. There's a corner building on a bit of a street just before the intersection with rue Dauphine. The apartment's on the third floor. Monsieur Roussy, who's underneath..."

Stop.

My brain was running away and my tongue after it. He had started me and I wanted to confide everything to him: where I was born, how my father and I used to drink milk in the kitchen when I couldn't sleep, and how my father would tell me stories, and about Agate crossing the street to speak to me, and Crevecoeur stopping outside my bedroom door and saying how much he enjoyed my company and he was just next door if there was anything I wanted in the night, and that I bloody knew I hadn't been in the white cube over a week because this was only Day Four, and that I was smarter than him because I knew he wasn't God behind that white light because if he was God why did he have to ask these itty-bitty questions? That was smart, I'd got him there. I'd save that, spring it on him later.

"You were going to tell me about Monsieur Roussy."

Yes, I wanted to. I was pleased he was anxious to know.

"Monsieur Roussy does not like men hammering on the ceiling. They said they had come about the carpet and that was a lie, wasn't it? They had come because of Agate and you know it."

Oh God.

Interrogator: "You mentioned Agate's name. You want to talk about Agate."

My brain had a million thoughts before he finished talking. I hadn't prepared myself for the drug. I forced my brain to go back over what I knew, forced it against the inclination rising in me. The drug could have been in one of three groups: hallucinatory (like lysergic acid) or stimulative (one of the amphetamines) or sedative and hypnotic (the barbiturate group). I had simply assumed the last, being the more commonplace. I had been wrong; I would have known and prepared myself if I'd paid more attention. The drug-administrator had taken the hypodermic out of my arm but if it had been Pentathol or Cyclobarbitone he would have left it in, drip feeding, but never letting me go fully under,

110

keeping me on the edge of consciousness while the questions came and my willpower collapsed.

My brain raced. There was no drowsiness, no hallucinations. It was an amphetamine—I didn't know which and it made no difference. Because they were bloody clever. Solitary confinement, trying to persuade me it was eight days on my own, programming me with sounds because the imagination provides its own horror pictures and that's much more powerful. Pumping me full of a stimulant because they knew I was desperate to spill all the things in my mind after being so alone.

Interrogator: "Agate came to see you." It wasn't a question, it was gentle prompting.

The light seemed brighter than ever. It was bursting into my brain. I closed my eyes and still I saw the light.

I said "Where are you? I want to see you. Please."

"What I look like is not important. You want to tell me about Agate. He was working for the Americans, right?"

There was sweat on my hands and forehead. I was bursting to reach him.

"He worked for the Agency. He was attached to the American embassy in Paris. Before that he'd been in Ankara, before that the Far East."

I stopped and my emotions soared in triumph. He'd said: *Agate was working for the Americans.* He didn't say: *working for us.* Deduction: I was not being held by Americans. He'd given himself away, he'd given everything away, because I was smarter.

Interrogator: "What did Agate tell you?"

Stop. My voice roared inside my skull. They've pumped you up and you feel big and powerful. You're a fool, you're not smarter, you never believed you were being held by the Americans. Stop deluding yourself, because delusions kill.

"Cody, I'm waiting."

I knew it wasn't the Americans holding me because there were only two options. If Ladouceur had disappeared, either the Agency had kidnapped him or he was an American under-cover man falsely "exposed" by the Agency to destabilize France—and that was pure Duraine. There *couldn't* be any other reason.

"Cody, I cannot afford to wait long."

The light overwhelmed me, it was the unbearable brightness of the face of God. I tilted my head and a camera stared down.

"Speak."

"Agate told me nothing. He was killed before he could speak.

111

Those bastards Duraine and McKosker finished him off."

"But you want to tell me more than that."

I wouldn't. I mustn't. If they knew everything inside my head, I had no more reason to be kept alive.

"Tell me what you know about Ladouceur."

Talk. Anything. Talk down the drug.

"There was blood on one of her nipples and I kissed it off and was stroking her belly, my fingers trailing down through the forest. Her name was Forrest, Dee Forrest."

"You are lesbian? But how about your friend Dolbiac?"

"Canuck, I'm sorry. If only you'd told me."

"Has the CIA ordered you to observe Dolbiac?"

"I would never be a 'bed and board'."

"We know he was a member of the Parti Québecois in Montreal before he came to Paris."

"He was an artist, a composer. He was brilliant, I never understood him. I shan't hear him play again. Canuck, I weep for you."

I wanted the tears to come and they wouldn't.

"What do the CIA suspect?"

"How should I know? Ask them."

"I'm asking you."

"I don't know. I'm not working for them. You'd never get me inside a core office in the embassy. Do you know the core offices each have the prefix C. There's C1, C2, C3, and on and on, world without end, that's my prayer, amen."

I swallowed. I was panting.

"Don't lie to me. We know all about you. What did Agate tell the CIA?"

I stopped myself. It would have been another denial, don't know anything. But my brain caught at it: *What did Agate tell the CIA?* The words seemed wrong. Agate *was* CIA. Wasn't he?

My brain raced as I dragged the pause out. How much real time passed, fifteen seconds, thirty seconds?

Interrogator: "Cody, you're being stubborn. We need to know to complete our files."

That was a lie. Their files are never complete.

My brain sparked, brief flashes trying to illuminate his words and then the darkness descending again. *What did Agate tell the CIA.* I couldn't grasp it. If Agate was going to tell the Agency something, it would be about the destabilization, and did that mean it wasn't an American operation? But it *had* to be.

I said: "I don't want to be in anybody's files. Now Crevecoeur has a file with my name on it."

"Is your job liaison between Crevecoeur and the CIA?"

"I don't work for them."

Something changed in the light. The intensity was less agonizing and I had a beautiful thought: the change was in me, the drug had peaked.

"You are going to make me angry. We know you are CIA because we have records of everybody who was trained at Langley."

I shook my head. When I closed my eyes, there were stars dizzying at the back.

"Talk."

"Oh sure, they trained me, but I quit. There was 'Aunty', he was the best. He set our group the week-end task of penetrating the White House and I was the only one who did it. Imagine. I came back with Nixon's signature in the front of Lenin's *Imperialism: The Highest Stage of Capitalism* and do you know how I got that? Do you know? You'll like this: I hid the book with the cover of Nixon's *Six Crises.*"

"Cody, keep to the point. What do the Americans know about Ladouceur?"

There was still danger, but I'd won. I could tell from the tone of his voice: it betrayed he knew I was on the down curve.

"Cody, there is no point in keeping the information about Ladouceur to yourself because it's too late. Do you understand? It is too late. You have been under observation for ten days and the election is over. Your information is of no further value to your superiors. We only need it for cross-reference in our files."

He even lied about the number of their false days. The situation was still critical: the election was the vital date.

For the first time I felt strong enough to tear my eyes away from the bright white light. I caught the frown on the face of the anaesthetist.

Interrogator: "What was the CIA plan to counter Ladouceur?"

It was his last throw and he didn't care what he gave away because I wouldn't be allowed out alive. It was positive confirmation: the Agency wasn't running Ladouceur. My brain was in turmoil, unable to work out reasons.

"You must talk."

I shook my head. "Why don't you try more dope."

"There are other ways."

Because he knew more dope wouldn't work either. There'd be

113

incoherence and screaming, the mind finally blowing its self-control. And no matter how long I screamed at him: *I know nothing, I have no connection with the CIA,* he wouldn't believe it.

"About Ladouceur..." the voice began.

I said: "If the election is over, tell me who won."

There was a pause while he was assessing. I turned my head and saw the orderlies still two paces behind. The anaesthetist stepped forward, reaching out to feel the pulse at my wrist.

"Take your hands off."

The light of the big opaque plate glass switched off.

The interrogator said: "You are going to regret not cooperating."

There was no threat in his voice. He was stating a fact.

I was returned to the white cube and left on my own. I was drained and forced myself to activity.

I set out scrutinizing everything for markings: sheets, pillow, coverlet, anything to tell me what country I was in. The coverlet showed a trademark in one corner—a sheep in a chemical retort—that I didn't recognize. The basin and toilet had no manufacturer's stamp. The aspirins concealed behind the toilet were anonymous. No marking on the taps, no name on the video camera. Then I thought of it. The lights in the ceiling were out of reach but by standing on the basin I was close enough to inspect the bulb. The brightness scarred the retina and left a searing pain, but I saw it: NARVA Berlin DDR.

I was in East Germany.

They brought a tray. I wasn't hungry because of the appetite-depressant effect of the amphetamine. My body clock had been upset. I forced myself to eat because food was necessary after the hypertension.

I had my thoughts for company. I was in some institution of the MfS in East Germany, but it could be the Russians interrogating. Beyond that I could make no coherent pattern out of Agate's death, Ladouceur's project and disappearance, the revelations and political reactions, the interest of French security and of the KGB in what I knew. I am politically naive or I might have made a connection; even so I would have rejected it as drug-induced wanderings.

The door was unlocked and the two orderlies came in.

The voice from the ceiling said: "You will accompany them."

14

It was an institute for the criminally insane. They were running it.

I stood between the two orderlies at the top of a staircase and watched the man cross the vestibule below. He stopped to have a word with someone carrying an old brown briefcase. They laughed and separated. The last trace of the smile was on his face as he came up the stairs, and it faded as he stood in front of me. What kind of sense of humour would such a man have?

The light twinkled on the steel rims of his little round spectacles. His eyes peered through with the steadiness we look through a microscope.

"You're being childish." The interrogator delivered the rebuke without emotion. He'd watched me for days on monitor screens but his gaze searched my face and body. When the eyes rested on my face again it was as if someone had tapped a hole in his skull and let the soul escape. There was nothing in the eyes behind the lenses.

"All right," and he nodded to the orderlies. He turned to keep me in view as I was led away. I think he'd just wanted to see me close to. It wasn't sexual: it was the appraisal of an abbatoir manager at a livestock auction.

I was in a different cube, absolutely empty except for the camera and loudspeaker in the ceiling. There was a glass panel in one wall and I assumed that was where I would be observed from. I was wrong.

"Cody," the interrogator's voice came from the speaker, "go and look through the glass."

I looked, and closed my eyes. My back was to the camera and I kept quite still, not wanting to show anything of what I felt. I checked through the glass panel once more, and waited.

"The dog is about two years old," the voice said. "No particular breed, a bit of terrier, a bit of sheephound. The only distinguishing feature from a million other mongrels is that the dog is rabid.

There are two forms of rabies in dogs: dumb rabies, when the animal largely lies still, and mad rabies. Watch."

I looked again, briefly, and turned to face the video camera.

"I'm not looking any more."

In mad rabies the dog runs round snapping at objects. This one's eyes were distorted, its jaws open. It had run in a small circle, snapping at the shadow cast by the ceiling light, tripped over its uncoordinated feet, bobbed up again, its narrow head raised and jaws chattering as if trying to catch a bothersome fly. The glass panel was double, with an acoustic gap, and I was grateful there was no sound from the animal.

But I could not stop the sound of the interrogator's voice. It was precise, a schoolteacher faced with an awkward child. I decided he was not Russian but German after all, because during the last war some of the worst of the Waffen SS officers had the same voice. They would be detached and punctilious in their orders, and the smoke bombs would be dropped in the sewers and the buildings set on fire and the machine guns would grow too hot to touch in the streets of the Warsaw ghetto; and in the officer's dining room the same precise tones would complain that the wine was incorrectly chilled.

"The next stage will be when paralysis sets in and the dog can only crawl. By tomorrow evening it will be dead. We have others. Also we have a wolf with rabies and that is more dangerous. Bites from dogs only pass on the disease in some fifty per cent of cases, contrary to popular belief, but the bite from a wolf is invariably fatal. You show no symptoms at first, not usually for five or six weeks and it can be as much as two years. Then you become melancholy and irritable. You feel restless, and within forty-eight hours the disease has completely gripped you. You display wild terror. You cannot eat, drink or swallow your own saliva. Even the sight of a glass of water thrusts you into a paroxysm of fear and revulsion. Breathing becomes difficult. Convulsions and bouts of maniacal excitement come more frequently. Finally, after about four days of agony, you die."

I stood gazing at the camera so that he could see my face, see that there were no emotions on it, neither fear nor loathing. I did not want him to feel he had control over any part of me: neither my body nor my mind nor my emotions.

After the pause he said: "Now I have three questions for you. Who is your Director at the CIA? How much of the Ladouceur project did Agate tell? What counter-action is the CIA initiating?"

116

I gazed at the glass eye of the video camera. It stared back, cold, unblinking, like his little round glasses.

"If I answer the questions, will you let me go free?"

"Provided you answer truthfully." He was too well trained to betray eagerness. His voice was flat, but he was lying nonetheless.

"One, I do not work for the Agency therefore I have no Director. Two, I do not know what Agate had to tell, because he was killed. Since what he had to tell was about *your* project, I assume it was your organization that acted to prevent him talking. If you are now ignorant, it is your fault. Three, the same answer as to the first question: I don't work for them, I don't know what they're doing."

I had angered him and his control snapped. "You stupid woman. Guards!"

And I thought: when they push me through the door, my only hope is to pull one of them after me. If I keep stone-still and the orderly panics, it will be his movements that attract the dog.

It had made no difference what answer I'd given because if the interrogator once believed some fiction I made up or believed the truth that I knew nothing, there would be further purpose in keeping me alive.

The orderlies entered and I decided on the one on the right because the other one had broader shoulders that were more likely to tangle with the doorframe. But when we went out of the room, we turned away from the rabid dog next door.

At the end of the corridor I was taken into a control room with a dozen TV monitors, three of them working. One screen showed the empty room I'd left, the second showed the rabid dog rolling on the floor scratching at its throat with its front paws, and the interrogator stood with his arms folded across his chest and simply moved his index finger at the third screen.

"Look."

It was a poor-quality picture, all shades of grey. A technician at a console in front of the monitors moved a knob and the camera did a slow zoom into close-up. The interrogator's eyes were on my face, evaluating my reaction, and I was determined he should have nothing to help him.

The man on the TV screen was grey, grey hair, grey skin, grey clothes. It looked a long time since his life had any colour in it. He spat on the floor and his hands went to his throat and then the spasm began. It was as if he was trying to tear a throttling collar away, but his shirt was open-necked. He made a sound, a dry short cough like a leopard's in the bush at night. His eyes were wide and they saw some horror I could only guess at.

"Show her," the interrogator said.

There was a jug and glass by the console. With deliberate slowness the technician poured a glass of water close to a microphone. The man jerked towards the sound coming from the loudspeaker, trying to scream, the sound coming choked. I watched his convulsion under the interrogator's gaze.

"He was stubborn," he said. It was an epitaph.

I counted to twenty before I spoke to him, wanting him to wait.

"Doctor Heuss, you're famous for these experiments, aren't you?"

"Not Doctor Heuss, I'm Doctor..." He stopped. "It is no concern of yours."

I studied him closely, wanting to remember his features if ever we met outside. He and my father had sworn the same oath.

"They had doctors at Belsen and Buchenwald and Ravensbruck too, didn't they."

He controlled himself because the orderlies and the TV technician were present.

"You must understand that once a person exhibits the symptoms of rabies, there is no saving him or her. The vaccine course has to be started at once during the incubation period, and the injections are painful. Think about what you have seen. I have more important matters than you to consider tonight. In the morning I am confident you will co-operate. It will be the final chance. Thereafter you will be living with a time bomb in your blood stream, never certain when the first rabies symptoms will show and it will be too late to save yourself. The death is long and excruciating."

"If I have to die, I prefer it to be quick."

"You cannot choose," he said. And then, the worry implanted in his mind, he turned to the orderlies: "Check her room, check everything thoroughly, make sure there's nothing she can use to kill herself. I hold you responsible."

I passed one window on the outside world on the way back to my white cube. It showed snow-covered fields to a flat horizon. The sun, weakened by the coming winter, hung above some farm buildings a kilometre away.

I would have to leave that night.

118

15

The frost bit deep into the ground and by dawn, if I were still free, it would claim my life.

In central Europe they take pneumatic drills to the graveyard in winter and I understood why. The frozen earth won't receive the dead.

The cold was like the steel of a knife on my face. I got to my feet and moved away from the shelter of some nameless bush. There were no sounds.

It was now four or five minutes since I had left my white cube and I wouldn't have much more time before pursuit began. Full darkness had just descended and when the moon rose my tracks would be totally visible in the snow. But that would hardly matter. They would use dogs, and dogs follow their noses not their eyes.

I would have to plan *now* for the dogs.

I was less than a hundred metres from the institution, headed in the direction of the farm buildings, when I discovered why there had been no security more efficient than a head-high wall topped with roller-spikes. The wire tripped me and as I sprawled the flood-lighting came on, all round me, and from behind there was the distant sound of an alarm.

My left ankle buckled with pain as I got to my feet but it wouldn't have mattered if it had been broken: I would still have run. I felt the sweat start on my body, not because of the physical effort but because the noises had begun behind me. They must see me. I was wearing an orderly's white coat but my hair and legs and shadow would stand out against the snow.

A hundred and fifty metres from the institution I met a track that ran parallel to it and this was my only chance. I thought there were half a dozen of them, but once there are more than three dogs it is difficult to estimate their number accurately. From the sound of it they were circling the institution searching for my exit point and when they picked up the scent they would be after me. I would be able to tell: the note of their barking would deepen.

If the interrogator had not been so worried that I would find some way of killing myself, getting out would have been a more serious problem. But the orderlies had searched and turned up my cache of aspirins and after that anxiety made them incapable of thought.

There is always a way to find death.

In jail they take away belt, shoelaces, tie; but that doesn't go far enough. They should take away underclothes because pants can be torn in strips and used as a noose. The prisoner should be entirely naked, but even that doesn't go far enough. It requires only willpower to force the end on yourself. I could have stood on the basin and dived to strike my temple against the rim of the toilet, impacting my brain at the weak point of my skull.

I drowned myself.

There was no plug in the basin in case I'd used the chain on my neck or against one of the orderlies. But they hadn't thought to remove my bra and I used it to block the plughole in the basin. The positioning of the camera was critical. As a small concession to privacy it did not cover the area of the ablution cubicle that contained the shower, toilet and basin; I was relying on this fact and the orderlies' reinforced worry about me.

I turned on both taps and watched the basin fill. Water spilled on the floor and I thought the timing would be about right: I had been in the ablution cubicle for three minutes and they would be staring at the monitor screen impatient for my return. The lake grew larger, reached the tile surround to the shower, and blocked in that direction began its move towards the room.

They would be watching the entrance to the ablution cubicle. I knew that because I'd risked a backward glance as I went in and the camera had followed my movements. How long before the tide of water flowing across their screen registered?

Success.

Their command of English was poorer than the interrogator's but over the loudspeaker I heard one of them say, "What are you doing in there? Come out at once." There was some sort of exclamation, Russian or German, and they were on their way. They would be running from the control room, desperate to save the drowning woman and avoid the interrogator's wrath.

Because of the anxiety implanted by their superior, I thought both would come. If only one came, the other would be watching on the monitor and the alarm would be raised before I had even reached the corridor.

I risked ten seconds at the entrance to the cubicle, using the bar of soap on the wet floor, rubbing until it became a skid pan, and then I knelt in front of the basin. Running footsteps, two pairs, and I plunged my head under the water.

Their view from the door would be of my legs on the floor and, further into the room, of my head slumped in the overflowing basin. I was killing myself, the very thing they had been warned against, and the thought obliterated caution.

The first one had no chance. His foot hid the wet soaped patch of floor and he ended his progress with his head against the hard ceramic pedestal of the basin. He made no sound. The second man was stopped at the doorway and perhaps he had suspected some trick. I stood up to face him, hands loose by my sides so he could see I had no weapon. He could have slammed the door on me and gone to raise the alarm, but no KGB or MfS guard would risk the humiliation of getting help to tackle a single unarmed woman.

He was left-handed. He came forward with his right hand shielding his genitals, his left hand held rigid to deliver a disabling chop to my windpipe. His gaze was fixed on my face, watching for the movement of my eyes that would warn of attack.

His comrade was motionless on the ground. I tried flicking my glance down to the prone figure but it had no effect on the eyeline of the other. He stepped closer, circumspect but confident.

At two paces I exploded, my breath forcing out the mouthful of water in a fine spray full in his face, and his reaction in blinking and raising his arm was pure instinct. I jump-kicked with my leg straight, full force: the side of my shoe landed on the ribs under his heart.

The sole criterion for selecting KGB guards is physical toughness. The blow didn't stop his heart but when I felt his pulse it showed an irregular beat and I decided he would be unconscious long enough for my need. Removing his coat was the most difficult part but I wanted some slim disguise if I met someone in the corridor.

The corridor was empty. The window at the end had metal shutters but no bars. I had to use a foot on the lock of the shutters and the sound crashed down the corridor. Nobody came; perhaps they were accustomed to the sound of bodies crashing within these walls. Hanging from the sill I had a drop of four metres to the frozen ground.

At the track I turned left, running crouched from the floodlights that stretched out to me from the institution. After a hundred metres there was a giant oak tree and beyond it a copse of pines that would offer some protection to a fugitive. I rejected the pines. I circled the trunk of the oak and retraced my steps to my original start point on the track. I jumped across and down into the ditch on the far side of the track and made some progress away from the oak when I heard the baying switch to a lower register. I lay flat in the ditch, scraping snow over my legs and hair.

It is hard to lie still and do nothing. Instinct tells the body to get up and run.

The dogs came to the track and turned left, following the trail I'd laid, with two armed guards behind them. When the dogs reached the oak they circled round, baying up at its branches. The guards reached the tree and I could see them peering up where its trunk forked, shouting, with the dogs snapping and barking. They had a small flashlight and couldn't be certain, because the oak is the last tree to become winter-bare and it still held a few dead leaves. Even when they did conclude I wasn't up the tree, I knew they would waste time quartering and searching the pine copse.

There was the sound of more raised voices at the institution and now instinct wanted me to repeat the successful action and burrow into the cold earth to hide. I clambered out of the ditch and set out towards the farm building. I estimated ten minutes before the dogs were brought back along the track and cast round to pick up my scent again.

He was only a boy, twelve or thirteen, and I felt suddenly numb that I was going to have to bring a kid down.

He looked at me from the entrance to the barn, and the light from the uncurtained kitchen window of the farmhouse slanted across his white face. The expression was tight, showing no fear but no expectation of anything good. At twelve life should not have closed in.

A kilometre behind me the institution and grounds were bathed in light and there was the sound of the dogs searching for my track. A voice called out an order and it drifted over, thin in the cold still air.

I could afford no more time.

"Russians," I said. *"Russische."* And then miming a gun, "Bang

bang bang—*kaputt,"* exhausting my vocabulary. I was breathing hard from running.

There was a moment's stillness, his eyes on me, and I knew if he yelled out I was too far away to reach him in time. I half expected the indrawn breath and the open mouth, but nothing came.

He gestured to me, turning to go in the barn, and I followed, thinking it might be a trap but that if it were he would have ushered me in first and slammed the door. There was a tractor, a trailer filled with some root crop, oil drums, a harrow, a coil of rope, some hand tools, and I could see no sign of his father with a shotgun. I saw the bicycle and then the boy was lifting down an old overcoat and putting it on me, covering the orderly's white jacket. I said "Thank you", and *"Danke schön",* and didn't know whether to kiss him or shake his hand. There was no way in which I could repay him, either for the bike or the risk. I smiled briefly and he stared back. I got on the saddle and pedalled down the rutted track away from the farm. Our lives had touched for two minutes. The boy had said not one word.

There is no iron curtain between East and West Germany.

It is barbed wire, electric fence, fragmentation mines, automatic fire guns with tripwires. The border guards in observation towers are there to record crossing failures.

There are mouseholes in the wire. The people who make the crossings don't see themselves as heroes. They have weighed the chances of success, know their little patch, can sniff where changes in defences have been made. They bring out a package, a human package, but it is without bravado and without publicity. There is no café you can go to, ten kilometres from the border, and listen for a whisper of an escape network. No games are played.

Still, the border has its attractions. You can see safety.

Instead I went east, heading in the direction of Poland and the Soviet Union. I abandoned the bicycle under a tree before the main road, where by now the *Volkspolizei* would be stopping everything on wheels. The country was flat but I had at last dipped below the level of the floodlit institution. My ankle was swollen, my stomach was empty, my head throbbed and I had no money. I was no longer concerned with the dogs. In the morning there would be helicopters.

I went across snow-covered fields, hard going with the furrows from the autumn ploughing solid with frost. I forced my pace because I had no illusions. I had been picked almost by chance and because of my past to receive information from Agate, a CIA agent. There had been two attempts to shut my file. My interrogation, like all interrogations where it is assumed the subject will not get away to speak, had told me a little too much to live. Ladouceur's disappearance had been set up by Moscow, its earth tremors were felt in France. Nobody had explained *why*.

I would relay my scraps of information to Crevecoeur, to the Agency even. They had analysts; let them work it out.

The overcoat the boy had given me kept me alive. When the moon came up I could see to walk more easily, leaving tracks in the snow that would jump out at a hedgehopping helicopter at daybreak.

I heard dogs but they were at farmhouses, not in pursuit.

It must have been midnight when I reached an autobahn and knew my escape was taken seriously. Away up to the left were two parked police cars and a man with a swinging lamp was stopping cars and overnight trucks. I was able to choose my moment, sprinted across the four lanes, lay on the ground clutching my ankle, and tried to remember what it was like to have warm hands. I came to the railway track after another hour.

As far as I could I had kept an east-west axis, at first using the position of the institution as a reference, and then the moon. During training I had scored relatively poorly at night tracking, but I have a strong will to survive. I turned north up the track. I came to what I was searching for: signals on the line. There were green lights at track-level, which I smashed with a ballast stone; the arm-drop signal above was too high to reach.

It was enough. The train came from the south, loaded with lignite, and it slowed because half the signals were blacked out. I caught the ladder on one of the hoppers and scrambled over among the soft brown nuggets on their way from the mines near Leipzig.

The train went slowly through the stations: Gräfenhainichen, Wittenberg, Luckenwalde. I risked an eye over the rim of my waggon in case I was running into trouble. Lamps cast pools of light on the platforms, there were Vopos in grey stamping their feet in the snow, but there had been no orders to search all freight trains. By dawn we were coming through the suburbs of East Berlin, the Fernsehturm visible in the pale sky. The destination of the lignite would be a power-station or fuel depot and when we passed a sign, "Berlin-Ostbahnhof 8 km", I jumped down.

The East Germans are the only ones who've made economic sense of communism. Among the leather jackets, the uniforms, the business suits, I looked a tramp in my dirty overcoat.

It was a long walk into the city centre, almost exactly eighteen months after my last visit. I'd sworn never to return to East Berlin. Now I felt a sense of familiarity, almost relief. Only the Wall to cross.

16

The movie had been called *Les Mecs méchants,* or some such. I'd only seen the title on the clapperboard, never outside a cinema. But I had watched, because what they were doing was for real.

This was the sequence. The camera was turning over, the clapperboard clacked, the director called action. Down boulevard St-Germain rolled the Citroen DS. The stuntman stepped off the sidewalk, was hit by the car, thrown to the ground like a broken doll. He rolled and lay still. The director called cut. The stuntman got up.

I watched the stuntman do it three times. He was unhurt, apart from scrapes on the palms of his hands. It was at his third attempt I understood the technique. We, the audience on the sidewalk and the audience in the cinema, were intent on the car and then the stuntman's raised arms and the shock on his face. We missed the feet, at the last moment sprinting to parallel the car's movement; and though he couldn't match the pace, he removed the worst of the impact from the bump. His roll across the road was little different from the relaxed fall every judo beginner is taught, only without the mat.

It hadn't looked easy, even when I knew how. He had torn a sleeve on take three, but that wouldn't matter with my old overcoat.

There would be no dry runs. I was going to get it right first time.

The point about Berlin is that it is still nominally a Four Power city. The 1972 treaty has given the west zone self-government and the east zone has become the capital of the DDR; but the fiction is maintained of Allied rights in the east. The Wall that went up in 1961 has been constantly reinforced until it is impregnable. Checkpoint Charlie and Friedrichstrasse station, the two holes in the Wall for foreigners, are subject to rigorous checks, and if your passport doesn't have the magic visa you'll be on your way to the MfS building in Normannenstrasse. But every day representatives of the three Western powers cross through Checkpoint Charlie to exercise their rights by cruising the east zone.

I'd seen them do it. I'd watched very closely eighteen months before and I had to trust nothing was different because I was in no position to check. I didn't think the pattern would be altered because that is not the way of the military mind, especially when the military mind grapples with international legal subtleties.

So, routine. The car, with a military driver and three officers representing the Allied Control Commission, would drive from the west zone. The East German border guard would approach the barrier at which the car stopped. The necessary identification would be shown to the *Grenzpolizei.* The Allied officers would not get out nor submit to a search of their persons or transport nor accept any visa—nothing that would imply they had not a right to pass this illegal border. There were three barriers in a zigzag configuration at Checkpoint Charlie. Then the Allied car was through. After the tour was over, the routine in reverse.

I had to do it so close to the border because nowhere else in the city would I be sure of meeting the car.

10 am.

I positioned myself behind the iron railings that protect the disused U-bahn station in Friedrichstrasse. I made a visual estimate of the distance to the last barrier of the Charlie crossing: about 120 metres. Part of the distance was occupied by a road which crossed at right angles. That was critical. It meant the Allied car would not accelerate until it was clear of the transverse road. Given the state of my ankle, I might run at 14 or 15 kph. If the car was doing more than 25 kph, my rebound would be too violent.

I prayed the legal tour hadn't been brought forward to 9 am.

There were no police closer than the barrier. By the hut and the pole figures in grey and khaki held automatic rifles.

A Berolina bus was crossing from the East. A BBS bus came from the West, American matrons wearing blue rinses, gawping at the windows and congratulating themselves on their bravery.

Two men came through on foot and one of them had a joke with a border guard. If I came through every day for a year, I would never smile at that point. Blood and hope had been spilt there.

I had crossed illegally before. But then I'd had weeks to organize the details and even so I had lost my rear windscreen and a tyre. Three times that night I had come close to losing my life. Once again I was under the shadow of the Wall.

I looked up: the sky was the texture of tripe in a butcher's window.

10.05. It came.

It was a Chevrolet, so I assumed a US Army driver. I was going to scare him. No one likes to run somebody down.

It happened quicker than I imagined, no time for fear. As the Chev approached the far end of the island, I stepped into the road from my position by the railings. He wasn't going fast and I had a split-second's anguish: *He'll stop in time.* Instead he pulled his right hand down on the steering wheel to avoid me, and I had to step further into the road before I turned my head to register horror on my face.

It was how Agate must have looked.

I raised my arms and managed to take half a dozen little steps in the same direction as the Chev, but I was never sprinting, and I got my hands down to the left side fender and with the bounce off the moving vehicle I did a roll and a breakfall on the tarmac that jarred the bone in my left arm from elbow to shoulder.

I wanted to rub the pain.

I wanted to cry out.

I lay dead.

The US officer was out first. There was Diplomatic Incident written across his face.

"Holy Christ, the stupid cow."

The railings hid me from the Checkpoint. If they were watching, they'd wonder why the Allied car had stopped.

"Oh God, if she's killed herself..."

So I leaned up on my good elbow and yelled, *"Espèce de con, vous conduisez comme un cbameau fou. Si vous aviez eu des yeux, vous n'emmerderiez pas tout le monde..."*

And more. I don't recollect. I let it flood out.

It brought the French officer. I was on my feet now and he'd no idea what hit him.

"What time do you cross back?" He looked taken aback and I cursed myself for slipping back to English. I repeated the question in French.

127

"About an hour," he replied. He was wide-eyed at my dirty coat and something about my face. He was past comprehension or questioning.

I stuffed the piece of paper in his pocket. "Leave the paper there. Read it after you cross back. Do what it says at once or the Sûreté will have your skin for lampshades."

There were four passers-by now, stopped, curious.

I think the French officer heard me but St Cyr hadn't prepared him for this kind of situation. He was looking bewildered and the American was plucking at his sleeve: "What's she say? What's she say?"

"The Vopos will be here in fifteen seconds," I told him. "Move."

I skipped on to the sidewalk and headed back to the centre of East Berlin. The pain in the back of my neck came from their eyes.

I was in the German Democratic Republic illegally, I had escaped from a security institution which would by now have circulated my description all over the country, I hadn't slept for thirty-six hours. But by evening two other considerations crowded everything else out.

The first was physical and there was nothing I could do about it because I had no money. Hunger was a particular problem, not because of pangs but because it is an indicator of a body losing energy and a brain with dulled alertness.

The second was psychological and I countered that as best I could. I had the desperate sense of being abandoned, not because I was alone but because of the attacks on my will. I had withstood days of solitary confinement, assaults on my body rhythms, threats of torture, drug manipulation, an unspoken but ever-present sentence of death. It had been all right when I was active. But in the period of waiting the emotion was overwhelming: I was abandoned for ever in a hostile country, without hope, with nobody to mark my going. My mind touched for a moment on the memory of Dolbiac. Even Canuck would not miss me. He would be in mourning for his own shattered life.

After all these decades survivors of Nazi concentration camps are starting to display the same symptoms. Their experiences of confinement, torture, degradation and threatened death were supportable provided they kept active. It is the 60- and 65-year-olds, when they retire, who are suddenly struck. The pain of being abandoned stretches out across the years and shows in their eyes and in the hands that keep touching lips and ears as if fearful of what they might be forced to say or hear.

I lost myself in humanity.

The Hotel Berlin-Stadt is thirty-nine storeys high and holds 2000 guests. No, 2000 numbers. I carried the lignite-smeared coat folded over my arm because they have standards to maintain. It was evening and I passed a line of patient tourists stretching from the door of the self-service restaurant: I had no money.

The magazine stall had all the news that's fit to read: *Neue Zeit, Pravda, Unitá, Morning Star, l'Humanité, Rude Pravo,* the rest. Any colour you like provided it's red. I circled the ground-floor reception area until I found it: a copy of *l'Huma* abandoned in a chair.

The French presidential election was due on Sunday and the prayers in ten thousand churches would be answered: the godless would be smitten down. *L'Huma* was raging against it.

I had just escaped from the dreamworld of some State Security Institution for the criminally insane. The rules had been quite clear to me: I would tell what I knew about the Ladouceur project and how the Agency intended to counter. And the interrogator hadn't cared that I therefore knew that Ladouceur's disappearance was a Soviet operation, because when my usefulness was at an end so would be my life. There was no controverting that.

And yet.

L'Huma had a primal scream at the world: *CIA accused. American imperialism in France exposed. Marchais asks: Is Ladouceur a prisoner at Langley?*

I thought they all were.

Headlines are a form of propaganda. I learned a little more from the story. The Soviet Union denied "holding" Ladouceur and accused the CIA. In the *Météo* column: maximum 0°C in Paris yesterday. Moscow said no work had begun on the river-reversal scheme and blamed American scaremongering for the hysterical reaction in France. There were power cuts in Metz and Lille because of renewed striking by electricity workers duped by capitalist lies. Fascist thugs had broken up more workers' meetings. An opinion poll putting Giscard seven points ahead was dismissed as "blackmailing the electorate".

The man came past my chair for the second time, and this circuit a smile got to work on his face. I got up and left. He could be a pickup. He could be from the Ministerium für Staatsicherheit looking for illegals in hotels, people without papers or changing currency. I knew he wasn't from Crevecoeur. I'd given him a rendezvous with twenty-four hours leeway to organize my crossing through the Wall.

I took the copy of *l'Humanité*. It's not only *clochards* who appreciate its insulating qualities. There were big white blocks of apartments south of Karl-Marx-Allee. I think it was the fifteenth car that was unlocked. I slept soundly, not because there is much room on the floor at the back of a Wartburg but because my body could take no more.

17

I thought he was praying.

He was dead.

His head was bowed on the steering wheel, the chestnut hair tousled, and he didn't move when I tapped on the glass. Then I saw the red staining his shirt and I opened the door and touched his neck. It is unnerving how quickly a body begins to have the coldness of the grave.

I could feel the dampness start on my forehead because this was the rdv: the ruined church off Köpernickerstrasse and within shooting distance of the Wall. That was another reason to worry: the bullet had been fired, not from outside the car, but from the I passenger seat and that implied an acquaintance. And third: it wasn't Crevecoeur but Pasquier. He'd had his last by-line in the *Courrier*.

I felt the hand fall on my shoulder and I didn't turn.

"Let's leave everything the way it is," Crevecoeur said.

We walked across the little square away from the Wall. There was a watchtower to the right but their eyes would be elsewhere. The covering of snow had been scraped from the paving in places: you could see the skid marks of boys' hands where they had packed it together to form snowballs. Some leaves crackled under foot but other sounds seemed to come from a long way off. It was my senses playing tricks.

"Won't he be discovered pretty fast?" I asked.

"What do you suggest? Drive up to Checkpoint Charlie with a dead body in the back? Phone the police? Call his editor?"

There was tension in his voice and eyes. I wanted to ask if he were carrying a gun and was it the one that had killed Pasquier. The eyes told me not to ask foolish questions.

"If you have East German marks," I said, "there's a café a couple of blocks away. I haven't eaten for two days."

"Does your ankle hurt?"

I'd forgotten the ankle, and the bruised bone in my arm.

I don't know who's responsible for restaurants and cafés in East Germany. Some are like canteens, others have a spurious air of *alte Berlin,* this one had come in a package off a supermarket shelf. There was a wealth of plastic. The chairs had spindly metal legs. Nobody would be allowed to sprawl across a table or shout to a friend. The waitress measured her welcome in coffeespoons.

The menu was typed. "I'll have the Russian egg."

"Oh yes," he said. You'd have thought my remark was significant. You could never learn what went on in his head from looking at his eyes, like cubes of ice in a forgotten glass.

I hadn't heard Crevecoeur step up behind me and it was an indication of how much my body had run down. He watched me eat the egg and vegetable salad, and then a pastry. The whipped cream in the pastry was real, so was the hot water in the coffee.

Crevecoeur lit a Gitane. I'd been missing the smell of French tobacco. "Who was it who said: 'Big nations make history; small nations receive it'?"

"You?" I suggested.

"Probably. France is a small nation, but de Gaulle and Pompidou had other illusions. Giscard too. Have you watched him during the election? His hands and mouth have been twitching, but if you know where to look you can see the strings. It has really been quite well done."

He played with the cigarette, rolling the tip round the ashtray.

"Listen. The French Military passed your message on to the rue des Saussaies yesterday afternoon. It went the rounds of the building and ended on my desk. Probably no more than fifty people had seen it before me. I was lucky to get a seat on the plane, I suppose. I told you before, we have no secrets from each other in the Sûreté Nationale." He gave me a smile with his lips. "You may have wondered why it was always Pasquier who got the stories first. He was being fed, the line stretching right back to Moscow. I just thought you'd like to know how he got to the rendezvous first."

"And was it you..." I stopped. It would have been a crass question anyway. But I stopped because of what Crevecoeur had said.

Four soldiers came in and sat at the table next to us. Crevecoeur had to slide along the bench to make room. Perhaps they were only conscript boys.

I felt the familiar clamminess break out in the palms of my hands.

Crevecoeur had his head on one side, watching me work it all out. He was playing with the Gitane packet, measuring its edges with long fingers, tapping it on the table, then turning it over and over as if he'd invented a square wheel.

One of the soldiers was staring at the packet and Crevecoeur offered them cigarettes. There was a round of *"Danke sehr"* and smiles, and the inevitable coughing at the alien tobacco, and it was my nerves stretched tight after the past ten days that suddenly snapped. I detested the way he set up tests and deliberately drew the soldiers into our circle when he must know the sort of pressures that had been on me. They're all the same. Ten years of duplicity and none of his kind would even be able to ask for the sugar in case it betrayed some secret part of his psyche.

"Stop playing your bloody games, Crevecoeur."

The soldiers looked at me because of the jangle in my voice and then away because perhaps they were intruding in a private squabble. But they were listening and I thought: At least Russian is the foreign language they learn at school now. And then almost at once: What did it matter if they understood or not?

"If Pasquier knew where to find me, he'd been told the rendezvous by someone in your office. Therefore every security organization from here to Moscow Centre knows where to pick me up. So why weren't they there? Why aren't I en route to the Lubianka? Why was it only you? I'm sick of your little deductions. You want to play God and watch me sweat out the answers. I'm sick of it."

Crevecoeur got out the small polythene bag they used to hand over the compulsory currency exchange and counted money out on the table.

"You're tired," he said. "We'll take a walk."

He was adjusting his coat, tugging down his left sleeve, and then we turned north. We crossed a bridge over the Spree, grey water reaching up sloping concrete banks.

"The life you lead is really very stupid," Crevecoeur said. "In fact so stupid I still find it hard to swallow. A fortnight ago I'd never heard of you. Since then I've been running the usual checks. Back from your *carte de séjour* form—family background, so forth. Exit cards filed at airports, flights to Madrid, Berlin, Istanbul, Milan."

There were posters; in East Berlin there are always posters. *Solidarity with our comrades in Africa. Resist American imperialism all over the world.* And there was a black and red one: *29 years of socialism in the DDR.* It showed three workers with fists clenched high: in France they'd be hurling stones at the CRS, in England they'd be voting to strike, here they were saluting the blood-red dawn.

I hugged my arms across my chest. The cold had penetrated right inside me. Crevecoeur had brought it with him.

"Then there was the question of what you used for money. A legacy I believe you told me?" He pecked a glance at me and went on with his evidence. "You have a checking account in Paris, small, and it didn't seem a total explanation. So I fill in the yellow form and wait. Switzerland, Lichtenstein, blank. But Luxembourg. An account with the Kredietbank opened eighteen months ago with a transfer of twenty-five thousand dollars. Two other smaller deposits: total of nearly forty thousand dollars. You do good business, Cody, good business with someone."

We were two old friends out for a walk. We could have been discussing holiday plans, or the kids' education, or someone else's infidelities.

"So we ran a trace. It turned out you had worked for our American friends—correction, been trained by them. But you quit on grounds of conscience, or some such."

He paused in his lecture. I knew without having to look that his head was half turned towards me. What could I see in his face that I didn't already know? There would be scepticism, irony, the assumption we shared a common standard of deception. You could see that face in every café in Paris. With so much natural talent, it's inexplicable the French don't have the best security system in the world.

"I could not believe it," he said. "You must maintain links, or be a sleeper. But when you ran into trouble behind the Curtain, you didn't cry for help to them but to me. It was a paradox. You truly are all alone?"

"I didn't cry for help. I don't belong to an organization and you do. Some things are easier that way."

The cold had driven all the pedestrians off Unter den Linden. Across the road was the Neue Wache where two soldiers paid tribute to the victims of fascism, goosestepping in unison.

"If you truly don't work for anyone, your life is more stupid than I could have believed," he said. "Why do you do it? You've got no cover, no back-up, no shields, no lifeline, no shoulder to cry on."

"You've left some of it out. No committees, no career men, no denial of personal responsibility."

He didn't want to hear that.

"Lonely on your own, isn't it?"

We're all alone, from the moment the umbilical cord is severed. We live alone, think alone, dream alone, suffer alone, die alone. Love is a frenzy not to be alone. In our passion we tear at each other, desperate to get inside the other, trying to be one body. We fall back, exhausted, and the sadness we feel is because we have failed, we are still alone.

Crevecoeur, for all the embrace of his department, was alone. That is the way they want it, of course. But he wouldn't acknowledge it to me.

"You said you wanted to know if anyone made contact," I told him. "They did. It seemed important that when I got out I should tell you what I had discovered. Since it was France it affected, I thought of you and the Sûreté. I thought you'd be eager, or at least willing, to help me so that I could pass on the information."

"Oh that."

I stopped to stare at him. "You're not interested?"

"You were kidnapped. You were held prisoner. You were interrogated by the Soviets, threatened with rabies. You told them nothing because you knew nothing. You escaped."

We looked at each other. Dolbiac had lost his reason for living. I had been kept in solitary confinement, threatened with torture, pumped full of drugs, hunted with guns and dogs. *Oh that*, he said.

"It's cold, isn't it," Crevecoeur said. "I think perhaps it may snow again."

"Ladouceur is going to make it snow?"

The smile, the mousetrap smile.

"People will believe anything, won't they. Come, we'll get cold standing here."

"I'm cold now," I said. "I want to cross over. We can talk on the other side. I don't like being the forward scout in the Cold War."

"We must wait for the arrangements," he said, and set off.

We were skirting Marx-Engels-Platz, past the bulk of the new Socialist Unity Party headquarters. Crevecoeur abruptly pointed up.

"Honecker sits up there, the third window from the left on the top. Did you know that?"

"Honecker?" I couldn't follow his thought process. My body was too exhausted and my brain was worrying about something else he'd said. "What has Honecker to do with it? He runs East Germany not France."

He shrugged. I'd seen him do it before. It was a movement of the shoulders that signified: everything or nothing.

We passed the Rathaus, monstrous red-brick monument to the nineteenth century. He looked at his watch and I tried to remember: was it the second or the third time? He took my elbow to guide me across the road.

"Agate," Crevecoeur said, running after a new topic. I was half listening to him, half heeding my own thoughts. Crevecoeur linked his arm through mine: we had become an old married couple now, united by our shared past. "I was surprised when Agate tried to see you. I knew he was an American agent, and doubling with the Russians. The Americans found that out and tried to turn him again. You know Duraine and McKosker, of course? Something you did in Turkey, wasn't it?"

Yes, I know them. And even if I didn't, even if I had never watched Duraine's little lizard eyes and McKosker balling his fist to conceal that half-nail, even if I had never met them, I would have known them. There are people like them in every security service in the world. I asked: "What time is it?"

"What?" He checked his watch. "A few minutes before midday. It was Duraine and McKosker who flew all the way over from Langley to squeeze Agate. I expect they were screwing him to find out all sorts of things about his Soviet contacts. But of course you knew that." He slid me a quick glance. He was always trying. "What did Agate tell you?"

And then I was certain what he was doing.

His eyebrows quizzed me. I said nothing. We'd crossed Molkenmarkt and some distance down Mühlendamm I could see a car drawn in at the side of the road, two men in front.

Crevecoeur said: "Poor Agate. The man who turns once turns traitor. The man who turns twice turns the tide of war. The man who turns three times turns mad. Who said that?"

"You."

He sighed. "Agate had turned mad. He was in that mental turmoil when he no longer knew which was home and who his friends were. He was desperate. And then he thought of you: you might help. If, that is, you weren't connected with our American friends."

"Let's slip down here," I said. Crevecoeur stopped at the entrance to the alley. It had a high brick wall on one side, a warehouse on the other. "Two boys from Memphis in that car down the road."

He frowned. "Memphis?"

"That's how the East Germans pronounce MfS. Haven't you heard Wolf Biermann's song? 'The Memphis Fan Club Blues'. One of the reasons they kicked Biermann out."

"You're worried about them?" The narrow face creased like a concertina.

There were a lot of reasons why cold clutched at my belly. I had a new one: they were my fingerprints on the doorhandle of the car with Pasquier's body in it.

"I don't like the way their eyes finger my body," I said.

Crevecoeur was smiling as we went down the alley. The idea I might be frightened of secret police was unacceptable. But he could appreciate the sexual reason. We passed a little wooden door into the warehouse and his thin lips were tight across his teeth. Kissing him would be like kissing razor blades.

I half turned to share his smile and delivered the jab under the rib-cage, full force, knuckles straight. The smile curdled. As he swayed down clasping his hands to his stomach I blacked him out with a chop to the check.

18

I checked past our wing and the MiG 21 was very steady, no more than five or six hundred metres away. Out of the porthole on the other side the sky was clear.

We disappeared into grey cotton wool, encountering the slightest of turbulence. I wanted to fly the whole way hidden in the clouds. Irrational. We weren't hidden: we were a bright steady blob on the radar screen in the MiG, a moving point on the screens in the control tower at Schönefeld airport.

We emerged above the clouds into sun, and sun brings hope. Best of all I could no longer see the industrial sprawl stretching out round East Berlin and Potsdam.

The south-west flight corridor runs from Berlin past Weimar and crosses the West German frontier heading for Frankfurt/ Main. It is the longest of the corridors, something over 300 kilometres. There was nothing to do but sweat it out.

The second officer appeared in the doorway and I asked him, "How much longer?"

"Slight tail wind," he replied. "Twenty-two minutes perhaps. I thought I should tell you, we've just picked up three more on the screen. They'll have put up from near Halle."

The French Air Force uses the Mystère 20 as a systems trainer and since detection of intruders looms very large in the life of aircrew I wasn't doubting he knew his job. But my nerves were no longer steady and I wanted more.

"Can't we lose ourselves?"

"You mean a snowstorm?"

That's massive interference of the MiG's radar, the snowstorm effect on their screen, and I hadn't meant that because they still know someone's causing it. I'd meant electronic invisibility, when the radar rays are not bounced back and your plane simply disappears off the opposition screens. But his eyes were steady on mine, and though he was younger than me, he'd learned to live with his secrets and this was one he wasn't going to give away.

"Mademoiselle Lamartine," he said, "we are on a properly filed flight plan with the approval of the East German authorities. Why should we become evasive?"

There were reasons. My life was one.

There are ten seats in the cabin of what is, in its civil version, an executive jet. There should be champagne glasses in the holders in the armrests, the smell of Havana leaf in the air, stenographers taking down business memos. Instead we sat side by side, Crevecoeur and me. I held his snub-nosed Colt .38 in the pocket of my shameful overcoat.

Crevecoeur said nothing.

Earlier, when his eyes had opened and he found himself in the dark of the warehouse down the East Berlin alley, he'd said I was mad. He was right. I was mad at him and all the people like him who felt my life was their property and all the secrets in it; and if I didn't know any secrets there was no reason for me to live.

You'll never get away with it.

He'd used phrases like that. So then I had said to him: "I want you to grasp this. I want there to be no misunderstanding in your mind. I am going back to Paris and I am taking you with me. And if anything happens and it looks like trouble, I am going to shoot you at once because I don't want to have any distractions while I try to save myself. I'll shoot you without hesitation, without any discussion of the ethics of it."

He was very quiet after that. It is bad to have an enemy in the Sûreté Nationale, so I reminded him: "When we're back I am keeping your automatic. It is the gun that killed Pasquier. It is my insurance." He had protested that I couldn't carry round the gun registered in the name of a Chief Inspector of the SN. "I'm not carrying it. It will be lodged with someone, explicit instructions in case of my unfortunate death. You're not getting your hands on it. You'd put a hundred rounds through and change the way it marks bullets so it would no longer match with the bullet lodged in Pasquier's chest. If I keep it, I would only use it once."

He had looked at me and I had nodded, pointing at his chest.

Three MiGs appeared on our left, the sun glinting on the East German markings. Underwing pylons held air-to-air missiles.

"How long?"

"Fourteen minutes," Crevecoeur said.

I had found the false passport in his inside pocket. Brigitte Lamartine, French citizen, public relations executive. The photograph looked like the one off the application form for my *carte de séjour.* There was no East German twenty-four hour visa in my passport nor in his and I had exploded, because you can't pass back through the Wall without it. "I didn't come that way," he had said. "I flew direct to East Berlin. I borrowed an aircraft."

The East Germans don't let Western military planes fly into their airports. Crevecoeur troubled me. It was the combination of a lot of things. He'd killed Pasquier—for being a good journalist? There was my false name and his unorthodox entry. In my mind it added up to this: There would be no record of my being in East Germany, no evidence of my departure.

The most troubling of all reasons had been his remark: *You were interrogated by the Soviets, threatened with rabies.* Who had told him? I hadn't.

We had taken a taxi to Schönefeld but away to the left of the civil terminal buildings past police cars and a detachment of army and even two T54 tanks with their noses sniffing at the French plane. I walked by the side of him and half a pace behind, my hand in the overcoat pocket. The two men in the prefabricated hut were in plain clothes. One sat behind the desk, the other stood against the wall. There was a framed photograph of Honecker on the wall and I could see the dust marks where a second photo had been removed.

"Tell them."

I'd spoken quietly though I felt far from quiet inside because I knew that in the normal way there had been no question of my returning to Paris with Crevecoeur. He had taken me for a walk in the streets of East Berlin having a last little chat before his midday meeting. Then I would have been passed down the line, first to the MfS in the car and then to the KGB. I would be an anonymous package sent to the Lubianka where they'd untie the string, unwrap the brown paper from my soul and prod around until they were satisfied as to what I did or didn't know. Their favoured end to interrogation is to sit you in a chair against the wall for a photograph, but the trapdoor behind opens and you get a bullet in the back of the neck.

At Schönefeld Crevecoeur had said there was a change of plan and I was being returned to Paris. There was, I suppose, the life of a big airport going on all round us, arrivals from Warsaw, Moscow, Havana, Istanbul. But this was our little world, tight, claustrophobic, where the movement of an eye seemed a large gesture. There hadn't been much conviction in Crevecoeur's voice and he was speaking to people whose profession was disbelieving. However the two men were MfS and there was a grey area of responsibility because Crevecoeur had arrived with KGB blessing, so in the end we got TO clearance. But with an escort.

"Six minutes."

I was watching one of the escort MiGs on the left peel off and disappear high up and behind us. There were a lot of explanations I wanted from Crevecoeur: about the Ladouceur project, why he'd disappeared, who was gaining what, his own position. But they were questions that could wait six minutes, or better still until we reached Paris.

Crevecoeur guessed my thoughts. "You can't do anything. The situation is beyond your influence."

"I want to do one thing, and it's the only thing ever since I've been involved in this," I told him. "I want to stop people trying to kill me. You're going to help me do it."

"You know, you're wrong about me."

I was going to tell him to knock it off when the second officer reappeared in the doorway.

"There have been a lot of signals," he said. "I think from Erfurt. They were coded so we're in the dark. Also, one of the Redbirds is flying on our tail now."

I knew Crevecoeur was thinking the same as me. The MfS at Schönefeld had been on to the "uncles" at Potsdam who in turn had checked with Moscow who had been furious at the stupid peasants for letting us go.

There was immediate confirmation. Our little executive jet lurched without warning to the right and began a swift descent, the noise of the engines changing as they were fully opened.

"Bon Dieu de bon Dieu."

The second officer was clawing at one of the seats to keep his balance and then his face flashed with the sheet lightning of terror. We followed his gaze through the porthole where there was a thin trail of something and then a short distance to left of us a giant firework display.

Our Mystère was curving away and down all the time, and the shock waves from the explosion were just so much additional thrust.

The second officer had disappeared and I hoped it was to play with the electronics. I was full of admiration for the pilot, for if he hadn't been watching the MiGs he wouldn't have known to throw the plane round; but he would be far too occupied with controlling the machine to worry about ECM.

The cloud cover was only a thousand metres below us. The note of the engines was rising and with the dive we'd be passing through the Never Exceed Speed before we reached the clouds. No sign of the MiGs out of the window but they'd be keeping well clear of the blast area. We were still in a tight curve and could have corkscrewed back in our original direction when the second missile came. The blinding flash was much closer and we knew it at once because of the sudden roar and agonizing pain in the eardrums as we lost pressure. My eyeballs were about to pop loose from their sockets and I saw a flood of dark red like a neon display had been thrown on. I sucked at the thin air and knew that if we'd been at 11,000 metres when it happened the pilot would have lost consciousness in the abrupt depressurisation.

The door to the flight deck banged open and I heard someone's voice shrill above the engine noise, *"Fous le camp"*, and I didn't know what or who he was screaming at. Perhaps he'd radioed Frankfurt and got a negative to his pleas for some Nato muscle.

There might have been a third missile, even a fourth. I couldn't tell. They wouldn't be satisfied with two unless they thought we were in a terminal dive. But the airframe was beginning to vibrate and I couldn't distinguish any near-misses.

I have no knowledge what missiles East German MiGs are armed with. The Soviet Air Force have Atoll missiles on their MiG 21s, and the really fast craft like the Foxbat will carry Acrid missiles with a speed of Mach 3.7 plus. But they don't necessarily trust their Warsaw Pact allies with all the top-drawer stuff because, well, you can never tell when one day you mightn't have to put an ally down. The missiles we'd been dodging couldn't have been infra-red or radar-homing; or else we'd been lucky they didn't score a first-time strike. Even Israeli pilots can't dodge the heat-seekers. Optical or proximity fuse, and the kill capability was not high. Langley would judge it 1950s technology. Perhaps I should let Nato know.

And then we were swallowed in the grey. The clouds would lose us, and if the second officer was doing his job we wouldn't be showing on their radar screens. They'd know we were pointing at the West German frontier but you can't shoot up clouds like you can depth charge the ocean in the expectation of a random strike.

Our Mystère 20 returned to level flight. Our height was about 2000 metres and the air in the cabin was cold and thin. It smelled good.

I remembered Crevecoeur. He sat with one hand to the side of his face. He was still and pale, and his eyes were half closed. His friends, if they were his friends, had just tried to kill him.

19

"I don't care what anybody *says*." I spat the last word. "I have had it up to here with lies, half-truths and deceptions. I want it proved to me."

That cynical partygoer had said I shouldn't trust organizations with three initial letters, but I knew IBM wouldn't lie to me. They might take over the world, but not deceive me. Computers had integrity, a quality lacking in everyone else I met. I didn't accept what Crevecoeur had told me in the car from the airfield about the Ladouceur project. I wouldn't believe Crevecoeur if he told me my mother's name.

The man looked taken aback by my vehemence. He checked with Crevecoeur, who just nodded. The man had said his name was Harvey, and I didn't know whether that meant Mr Harvey or good old pal Harve. But he was going to have a conversation with the omniscient computer at Institut 21 and that was what I wanted.

"Well, okay," Harvey said. He got a defensive look in his eyes as if I might destroy him if the answers came out wrong.

We were in the dust-free, humidity-controlled, constant-temperature nursery where the computer kept its soul. Tubes in the ceiling gave out an even, shadowless light. It was the kind of place where they might plan the end of the world, and probably had.

Harvey made a vague gesture at the control console and the memory banks. There was a glass panel in the wall and beyond someone was lacing up a big spool of tape as if this were a recording studio.

"This is the smartest computer in the world," Harvey said. There was no pride in his voice. "COBOL, APT, FORTRAN, it understands seven languages. But undiluted human language is beyond it." There must have been something in my face for he went on: "Don't be fooled by that parlour trick out on the sidewalk. You punch out a question there and we have a crewcut turn it into something this brute can digest and out comes your answer. It's not the expensive hardware that does it; it's the wetware." He tapped his forehead. "All I'm saying is, you cannot sit at the console and command: Tell me about Ladouceur's river-reversal project. That's about as sensible as swearing at the TV when it goes wrong."

I thought everyone swore at the TV when it went wrong.

Then Harvey took a good look at me. He wore round pebble-thick glasses, a striped shortsleeve shirt and a ruby in a signet ring on his right hand. He fitted into no neat pigeonhole: neither mad scientist nor technological genius nor undercover Agency man. He'd been subdued by my arrival with Crevecoeur, but now he sensed I was just another dummy overawed by computers.

"We have more data stored in our core than any other computer anywhere," he said. "This is the twentieth-century equivalent of the Renaissance Complete Man. Access and relationships are the twin problems. It is a question of the program, right? Organization of material, construction of a model, knowledge of what specific questions you want answers to."

It seemed best to nod. And then I realized he was waiting. I said: "I really just want to know the climatic effects of reversing those three Soviet rivers."

That was the key to the whole mess. It went back to what Pasquier had written: *There will be no more champagne, like shifting France two hundred kilometres north, every family will be poorer.*

"I don't think..." Harvey searched for words, "...that you really comprehend. This is not a closed analytic problem. This is a moderately complex stochastic problem. I mean," and he suddenly gave a human smile, "ask the right questions and the computer will have a damn good guess."

Ladouceur would have asked the right question.

If Ladouceur was the genius everyone made out and he had access to this computer, he'd have found out the answer to the fundamental question: Is the river-reversal project feasible?

Harvey moved to sit on an ergonomically designed chair on wheels.

"You'll have to take me on trust." He swivelled round to eye me. "I'll define the problems and produce for you the answers to a range of questions. But you'll have to trust I haven't already fed biased information into this tin can."

I nodded again. If the project turned out not to be feasible, Crevecoeur could be right and I had blocked a play in the Cold War game.

"Another thing. Watching a computer is one of life's less interesting spectator sports, and you'd never catch me cheating."

We left him. Crevecoeur had his pack of Gitanes out before the door hissed shut behind us.

A short walkway brought us to the centre of the building, different from the core of US embassies. It was five storeys above ground, five storeys below, and the inside was hollow down to the fifth storey below ground. It contained a garden like a lunar landscape, a fountain inside a glass globe constantly recycling mercury in a glittering shattering cascade. There was a statue tortured out of stainless steel (the plaque read: "21st-Century Man"), a cedar tree tortured by a Japanese, and tubular coloured lighting.

"This is called *le cratère*," Crevecoeur informed me. "Those banks of tubular lights are connected to the computer. You can choose any music from Scarlatti to Oldfield, the computer plays the synthesizer, and the correct tube lights up to each musical note."

Crevecoeur seemed at home. It was another thing I didn't like about him.

"The variables are these." Harvey had a stack of white cards on the table. He read from the top one. "Sea, land, and atmospheric pressure. We look for responses in temperature, wind and precipitation. And then we make projections into effects on agriculture, industry, macro-climate, marine life, communications, social behaviour, military posture, political stances and responses, economic cost and overall viability."

Harvey checked I was following the big words.

"Ladouceur didn't discuss this project with me or any of the other guys but there is no doubt he was working on it. I deduce that because there was some very esoteric data fed into the store-core. The notice on the street boasts the computer knows everything, which is kind of stretching the truth. It knows an awful lot, but Ladouceur had been exploring some strange by-ways. It's funny: a computer is meant to be so impersonal, but it suddenly gives out stuff that only Jean-Louis can have put in and I can almost hear his voice. He was a man who was interested in everything, you know."

Harvey tapped a card. "For instance, what conceivable effects there could be on the social life of Murmansk. This is the Soviet Union's only year-round warm water port in the Arctic, so it has immense strategic value. It's up on the 69th parallel and apparently is the twin city of Jacksonville, Florida. However, Ladouceur seemed concerned even with climatic influences on the *Praznik Cevera*, the reindeer and ski-racing festival held in late spring. I don't think you're interested in that kind of detail."

"No."

Crevecoeur had his eyes on me. I didn't look directly. I could tell from the angle of his face and his immobility.

Harvey dealt himself another card. "The basic scheme is to dam the rivers flowing north into the Arctic ocean: Yenisei, Taz and ObIrtysh; to create a vast freshwater lake; and return the water south and west for industrial and agricultural purposes. There is no problem with the technology of the dam and the canals

144

leading the water back; there would be problems of scale, but they'd be overcome."

He searched through the stack of cards, at a loss. "Look, we have to start somewhere. Let's take the effect of cutting off the rivers on the Kava, Barents and White Seas—they're bits of the Arctic ocean. Straight away we come to an apparent contradiction and we ask the computer for help. With less freshwater flow, the salinity of the Arctic ocean would rise and there would be *less* ice formation. On the other hand there would be less heat input from the relatively warm river waters and hence a tendency to *more* ice formation. Computer judgement: effects on the ocean environment would cancel each other out. But computer indicates error: the most important determining factor of ice formation has been excluded.

"The most important factor is the Gulf Stream. This starts off the coast of Florida—hey, that explains why Jacksonville is Murmansk's sister city—moves up the coast of America, across the Grand Banks, becoming the North Atlantic Current. It does nearly thirty kilometres a day up the Norwegian coast before branching into the Barents Sea. It is the most decisive factor in moderating the climate and permitting Soviet shipping to operate year-round without trouble from pack-ice. It is able to do this because passing North Cape the current sinks on account of its greater salinity and it continues as far as Murmansk. But suppose the volume of fresh river water flowing northward into the sea is stopped. What is the effect? Computer judgement: the undercurrent will flow up near the surface, dissipate its heat in the bitterly cold atmosphere much sooner, the pack-ice will advance south, Murmansk could be isolated for three or four months of the year; also the presence of warm water on the surface meeting cold airflows will mean increased fog, increased danger for surface shipping."

When Harvey turned his face at a slight angle, his eyes behind the thick lenses almost vanished. Then he would turn back to look straight at me and they were huge, hungry for scientific knowledge. He'd been diffident, almost embarrassed when we first talked. Now the fervour gripped him. He was the essence of the scientist, knowledge at no matter what cost. They'll always find people of his kind, I saw it in his hunger, people to work in laboratories doing experiments. And painkillers, nitrogen poisoning, poultry food, purification of the race—do they differentiate?

Harvey said: "The main Soviet naval base is at Murmansk on the Kola peninsula. This is the home port of the North Fleet. Nato is very concerned at the build-up of the submarine fleet which is deployed in the Atlantic and could sever the shipping links between America and Europe. There's a launching every six weeks. Submarines can pass under pack-ice and when it's not too thick can punch holes to fire missiles.

"But now comes a new situation: the pack-ice freezes deeper, missiles become inoperable, certain passages along the seabed out to the Atlantic become impassable, access to the pens at Murmansk becomes a serious problem. No military planner would accept the risk. Also there is another factor. The ship canal that links Leningrad to the White Sea has been upgraded to take ships as big as destroyers; this is because the main Soviet naval construction yards are at Leningrad. Computer judgement: this investment would be wasted if increased pack-ice meant the ships could not escape into the Atlantic."

In front of a captive audience an expert can be enthusiastic for hours. Harvey spoke from his little prompt cards dealt by the computer. IBM proved the Russians would be insane to undertake any river-reversal scheme. It would curtail the usefulness of the military complex in the Kola peninsula and cut the strike power of their North Fleet. (The computer also thought big. It produced a counter to this problem even more grotesque: the Soviets could dam the Bering Strait, incorporating a series of giant sluice gates; by allowing the ebb tide to flow south but restraining the flood it would subtract water from the Arctic and drag the warm Gulf Stream further across the roof of Siberia.)

It was almost a postscript. We reached our own little situation: the climatic effects on France and the electoral panic that had blown up. Computer judgement: if the cold northern waters were sent through the Urals into European Russia for irrigation uses, they would lower summer temperatures and increase cloud cover with negative effects on crop growth. This adverse effect would stretch across Russia as far west as the Polish border. Western Europe would not be affected. France would be untouched. Only Russia would suffer.

I didn't need the computer to tell me: the hysteria had been deliberately induced. Pasquier had been fed a rich diet of lies to put into the *Courrier*. He had been duped and manipulated, like the French voters. It was a move in the Cold War games.

146

This is what Crevecoeur had told me in the car from the airfield, what I'd wanted proved. Because it seemed beyond reason. I would not believe it, I could not believe it. To destabilize France and blame the communists might be a coherent play by the Agency. But I knew from the interrogation inside the East German Institute that it was a communist move, indeed they were neurotic that the Agency had a counter to the disappearance of Ladouceur.

A mad world, my masters.

Crevecoeur's eyes were watchful on me. I didn't look. I may have sighed.

Harvey said: "Finally, you can never say whether you want something until you know how much it's going to cost. Computer judgement: about 250,000,000,000 US dollars at constant prices." He ticked off the zeros on his fingers. "That is the initial stages. Maybe double or treble when you take in the associated costs of industrialization, new towns, communications, new defence needs, the whole caboodle. Who knows?"

Yes, Pasquier in his newspaper had been fed that figure, though not the final cost, because that was like trying to estimate the number of stars in the Milky Way.

Harvey became human again.

"If I may add a personal note, engineers underestimate the difficulties and the setbacks. You could probably multiply their estimate by a factor of three or four. Computer was asked for the effects of this vast sum on the Soviet economy. Judgement: it would absorb for the next two generations all additional created wealth, it would be the only area of economic growth. Looked at strategically: Soviet military spending and living standards and technology would be frozen at today's levels until the year A.D. 2040. Computer evaluation: totally unacceptable to any conceivable combination of leaders drawn from the Kremlin, the Soviet communist party, the armed services and the Intelligence apparatus."

Harvey poured himself a glass of water.

The Ladouceur project was destroyed.

I suppose I could have said thank you.

20

I had never been saluted by a cop before.

Crevecoeur bobbed his head in acknowledgement as we crossed the ground-level vestibule of the Institut 21; round the expensively designed girls at the reception desk, and we were aiming for the door to the street when the bomb blast came.

If the explosive had been placed in the entrance, it would have killed me.

If the explosive had been wedged so its shock wave was directed inwards, it would have killed me.

I felt the blast in my ear drums and in the soles of my feet and right up my legs and deep inside my belly; and there was the shudder of the floor and the swaying of the wall, though it could have been my eyes and brain that jarred and seemingly moved the building; and there was the wild symphony of sound, the drumming of percussion and the million triangles of glass showering everywhere; and the hot breath of wind blown from the Sahara.

It took a second.

I was falling to a prone position with the glass cascading round me.

My senses were sending a berserk jumble of messages. I heard Crevecoeur cry out something and the screaming began from the girls and there was still a hollowness in my ears after the terrible loudness of the bang. I smelled scorched plastic and cement dust and some chemical I didn't recognize. I tasted the dust too. I felt fear and I thought: Please God, will they never stop trying to smear me out.

Crevecoeur had been rocked off his feet by the shock wave; then he was scrambling up and pounding towards the entrance. He had his hand inside his jacket, though I was the one with his gun. The uniformed *agent* was making a pointless noise with his whistle and when I joined them outside there was the beginning of a crowd. They never seem afraid there'll be a second blast.

That's what the Irish Republicans do: a second blast to kill those trying to help the maimed and dying.

Whoever placed the explosive device would have vanished, but Crevecoeur was slamming from one sightseer to another. I think if he'd seen one with the least spark in his eyes, Crevecoeur would have felled him.

A graffiti artist had gone to work on the wall just beyond the gaping hole in the glass: *Ladouceur assassin.*

So it wasn't me they were trying to kill. It was a piece of mindless political violence, the kind that tries to solve a problem by killing it.

Then I saw the streak of red down my coat and felt the sting. A splinter of glass had lodged in my cheek.

We got in the taxi and he asked where I wanted to go. My brain was still in shock and I didn't reply. He gave the driver the Sûreté address in rue des Saussaies.

Crevecoeur looked at me and said: "You've been through a lot."

It irked me that it showed on my face. At twenty-eight you should be able to absorb everything and show nothing.

"I'll do one thing for you," he said. "I'll pass word to the people in Dzerzhinsky Square to leave you alone, that you've nothing to do with the CIA."

I looked at him. The shutters were down at the back of his eyes, but I thought if I were able to peep through I might find a trace of guilt. It was as near as he would come to admitting he'd put the Russians on to me in the first place. And the second place?

"Crevecoeur, you were going to hand me over to them in East Berlin."

"It seemed necessary at the time. We cooperate to an extent where our interests are the same."

"Cooperate? They tried to shoot you down in flames. They sent four MiGs."

"We all take risks." He shrugged. "If a Soviet missile doesn't get you, a madman with a bomb can." He jerked a thumb over his shoulder.

The taxi was making slow progress. I looked out at the late afternoon sky. Grey low-hung clouds, but I doubted it would snow.

Crevecoeur swung round. "You still can't see it, can you."

"No."

He said: "Here's this brilliant marxist scientist, working on a secret Russian project, disappeared. To the public, a mystery. To

149

anybody who's suspicious, obviously American agents have snatched him.

"But let's look through the other end of the telescope. Brilliant scientist disappears, mystery over his secret project, revealed he is working for the Soviet Union on a scheme that will have devastating effects on France.

"Now we know that's not true but nobody in authority has denied it. Certainly not the French government. Nor even the Soviet government. They have been careful to say they are not holding Ladouceur and the scheme has not started. No more. They must have been delighted when the early start to winter provoked public emotion.

"The public is gullible, they *want* to believe stories. That is the psychological basis that supports the Cold War. So the connection is made in the public mind: the comrades in France are no different from the comrades in Moscow and they are not working for the good of our country. Immediately Giscard's popularity over the Communist-Socialist candidate soars. Now, can you think of any reason Moscow should want that to happen?"

I said: "But Moscow can't want Giscard to win."

He said: "Is that what you learned in your East German cell?"

I tried to recall the exact words of the interrogator. *How much of the Ladouceur project did Agate give away? What counter-action is the CIA proposing?* Was that it? My life had been so twisted, my world turned inside out.

He said: "It's easy. Can't you see?"

Our taxi was stuck at a traffic light and it went red-green-red while we didn't move. The driver was cursing softly under his breath. Crevecoeur waited for an answer. He found me a poor pupil.

"All right. There is nothing the gentlemen in the Kremlin fear more at this moment than what is called Eurocommunism. It terrifies them, far more than the Pentagon. They shake when West European Communist Parties say they believe in plural societies, what a good thing free elections are, how dictatorship of the proletariat must be abandoned, how there must be a free press and free speech, and if the electorate votes them out they will go quietly. Cody, you must see that?"

He looked at me, almost pleading. Our taxi had moved to the next jam. A man with an armful of *France-Soir* did ballet steps between cars. Crevecoeur bought a paper. The headline said: *Tomorrow's election: Giscard will win 57-43.* He read no more.

150

"Think of Honecker sitting up there in his airless office in Karl-Marx-Platz. This is the best news he could have. I mean, the Russians sent in tanks to crush East Berlin in 1953, Budapest in 1956, Prague in 1968. If liberal communism became respectable and successful in France, how's Honecker going to hold the DDR down? It's a nightmare for Moscow. All the satellite countries would be flying into free orbit. There'd be bloody clashes all over Eastern Europe, outcries in the West. The world would be on the brink again."

He was hunched round, willing me to agree. My brain was stalled.

"Look, if you want more proof of how seriously Moscow takes this, look what they did to you. They were terrified the Americans would try to counter it. They killed Agate when he was turned again, they tried to kill you because they thought you'd found out, then they planned to torture you to see what the Americans were planning. Doesn't that convince you?"

The taxi braked hard and the driver muttered something about *les sales cocos* as a mob surged through the traffic.

Crevecoeur leaned back in his seat. "Your friends Duraine and McKosker must be delighted. They see the Russians ensuring the communists lose the election here and they don't have to lift a finger."

I shook my head. "It's so complicated, so unnecessary."

"Why do you expect the world to be simple? And it seems very necessary to them. Moscow has worked it out perfectly. Ladouceur is engaged on a Soviet project, so when he disappears the faithful round the world see the hand of American imperialism. But when the French voters hear of it, and it is presented just right, they turn against the PCF. An elegant manoeuvre. Let the present liberal leadership of the communists lose the election and be discredited. The hardliners will take over the party again."

Crevecoeur lit a cigarette, ducking his head down into the flame, frowning. And then, "My God, suppose Giscard feels this is the moment to reintegrate with Nato. The election after next is the one Moscow wants to win. Imagine: the first communist-led government in Nato."

It was like watching someone working with a knife on an onion: Crevecoeur peeled off layer after layer of deception and double-dealing. My cheek was hurting and I put a hand to it. "I hate conspiracy theories. They're just prejudice. You can't disprove them."

"Huh." He seemed to lose interest in me. He leaned over to the driver. "What's wrong with the traffic?" We'd taken twenty-five minutes and were only at Etoile.

"They've called a rally. I heard it on Europe Number One." He slapped the radio. "He's come back from Siberia and the Reds are showing him off."

"Ladouceur?"

"Bloody traitor."

"Where's the rally?"

"Rond-Point." It was directly on our route.

Crevecoeur frowned. You could see the pique: nobody had told him. And then the worry: it didn't fit his theory. They should keep Ladouceur hidden until after the election.

I said: "I can't grasp your motives."

Crevecoeur looked away through the window to the bare trees. He didn't like to undress his soul in public.

"I'm not in the pay of the KGB or the CIA. I'm right in the middle. We're one of the small nations, remember? We're a joke trying to make our own history. But when I see Moscow working to impose history on us and it's identical with what I want, I'll give any help I can. The Sûreté works for France, and from the Minister down we are agreed this is for the good of France. If two or three people get knocked over in the process, too bad. That's Cold War. And you," he faced me again, "you can see nothing but your tiny personal morality. Why are you so self-possessed?"

I was numb.

We sat, each nursing a private resentment, until Crevecoeur's patience snapped.

It was the noise.

Crevecoeur paid off the taxi half-way down the Champs-Elysées and we walked.

I was immersed in the noise and it was overwhelming. It was as if everybody in the crowd had been pumped full of amphetamines and was bursting with words. You saw crowds like it on newsreels and here I was part of it, in a little timeslice of history.

Crevecoeur was pushing at people because he was angry with me and worried about the unpredictability of the situation.

It was dusk and the lights came on. Ahead I could see metal scaffolding and a platform draped with red flags and huge *Votez* slogans.

They should have held the rally in place de la Bastille or place de la République. They are traditional rally-points and they'd have had a better chance of sympathy from the surrounding quarters. The crowd was mixed in its passions: a certain recipe for disaster.

There were placards: *US = SS, A bas la Coca-Colonisation,* and one cartoon of Carter with a peanut body and the caption *Président Caca,* and it was the Carter placard I saw go down in a knot of fighting.

"Where's the bloody CRS," Crevecoeur shouted. "They're never around when they're needed." And then, "Must have been ordered to stay out."

Crevecoeur eeled his way between bodies, making for the front, because he was afraid of the electricity in the air. Now we were a hundred metres from the platform where a bunch of people stood lit by spotlights and one grasped a microphone, the words spewing out of loudspeakers.

"...who has been the subject of a campaign of hate and lies, of fascist filth, the victim of an American imperialist plot to subvert the will of the French people, turn us against our..."

The crowd, the noise, the oratory, awakened echoes in my mind of running from unknown assassins and the glint of the long barrel in a street light, and then I thought of those newspaper headlines: *Un mort, 23 blessés.*

There were shouts, fists, two men went down and at once other bodies piled on top, kicking, punching, screaming.

"Do you know," Crevecoeur began and I had to duck under a huge torn banner to catch up with him, catch his words. "If Ladouceur were to die at this precise moment it would be the perfect solution: America would be happy, Giscard would be happy, Russia would be happy, and I can assure you..."

I lost the rest; I assumed Crevecoeur would be happy. He'd used the knife and another layer had come off the onion.

There were screams. A woman staggered past, blood streaming from a gash on her forehead.

Crevecoeur halted abruptly, sustained by some thought, rounded on me.

"You can see that surely? You're not too self-obsessed to see?" Among the vertical lines on his face was the question mark of an eyebrow. "Of course," he had second thoughts but the eyebrow didn't subside, "the propaganda victory would go to the Soviet Union because the rest of the world would think Ladouceur had

153

been kidnapped by the Americans, escaped from them, and been shot by them to avoid telling what he knew. But I think that would be acceptable to us."

Then he came.

There were indrawn breaths and people pointing and struggles subsiding. When we looked towards the platform, Ladouceur was climbing the steps.

He could have been kidnapped. He could have been held incommunicado in some institution for the criminally insane. He resembled his photograph, only older, with confusion written on his face, and a pallor that wasn't only the spotlights. He stumbled, and I wondered about drugs.

He stood uncertainly on the platform, looking bewildered at being present in a situation that was nothing to do with him.

He's a good man. Dee's words. She'd been insistent, wanting the words marked by someone. And the way she'd gone on to talk of him in the past tense. An epitaph: *A good man.*

"Comrades, I give you Jean-Louis Ladouceur."

Someone might have thrown a switch marked "lynch". There was a howl and chunks of the mob were battling to get forward and being met by the strong-arm stewards surrounding the platform.

The noise was terrifying again.

"Oh, it's very neat." Crevecoeur's words were snatched away in the uproar. And then to me: "You were a professional once, you'd appreciate the neatness of that endplay."

Up on the platform the puzzled overwhelmed figure put his knuckles to his cheeks and shrank behind the protection of his arms from the waves of hate and violence.

I looked round in the deep dusk. The crowd, the buildings, the roofs, the trees, and I thought: There are a thousand places, nobody would know where to begin looking, nobody would catch the glint.

Crevecoeur gave a narrow smile and did nothing.

Fear grew in me, for that hopeless, helpless figure on the platform. I felt pity for him, which no one else did, used, abused, tossed aside. I began to push blindly forward.

There were bodies, dense-packed bodies in my way, and they pushed back.

"Cody, wait." Crevecoeur was stumbling behind, his voice showing anxiety.

I got someone's elbow in the chest.

"Cody, don't be stupid, you'll only do harm."

I looked at the platform and he was still alive. The last speaker was lifting Ladouceur's arms up, like a champion acknowledging the crowd's adulation, lifting his arms high in the air.

Crevecoeur's hand clutched at me. "No one will believe you. You'll just be raving."

I swung round. "God, have you no..." No, he hadn't. I didn't finish.

And then there was no noise, nothing from the loudspeaker, nothing from the crowd. It simply fell away. I saw Crevecoeur's eyes go over my shoulder. They were ice-eyes, focusing beyond. As I swung back to face the platform there was a woman's cry, one.

On Ladouceur's chest there was a red star.

The crowd started. There were murmurs, ripples, a scream from near the front.

Crevecoeur's hand fell away from me.

"Oh yes," he said.

Ladouceur's hands gripped his chest and, as I watched, the red star began to flow between his fingers.

Other Top Notch Thrillers from Ostara Publishing

John Blackburn: *The Young Man From Lima*
ISBN 9781906288440
Brian Callison: *A Flock of Ships*
ISBN 9781906288358
Victor Canning: The Rainbird Pattern
ISBN 9781906288518
Francis Clifford: *Time is an Ambush*
ISBN 9781906288365
Francis Clifford: *The Grovsvenor Square Goodbye*
ISBN 9781906288433
Desmond Cory: *Undertow*
ISBN 9781906288624
John Gardner: *The Liquidator*
ISBN 9781906288464
Adam Hall: *The Ninth Directive*
ISBN 9781906288372
Adam Hall: *The Striker Portfolio*
ISBN 9781906288556
Geoffrey Household: *Watcher in the Shadows*
ISBN 9781906288457
Geoffrey Household: *Rogue Justice*
ISBN 9781906288549
Duncan Kyle: *Black Camelot*
ISBN 9781906288426
Jessica Mann: *Funeral Sites*
ISBN 9781906288600
Philip Purser: *Night of Glass*
ISBN 9781906288297
Geoffrey Rose: *A Clear Road to Archangel*
ISBN 9781906288303
George Sims: *The Terrible Door*
ISBN 9781906288280
Alan Williams: *Snake Water*
ISBN 9781906288310
Alan Williams: *The Tale of the Lazy Dog*
ISBN 9781906288341
Andrew York: *The Eliminator*
ISBN 9781906288563

All Ostara titles can be ordered from our website
www.ostarapublishing.co.uk **or from your local bookshop**
All titles also available from
Heffers
20 Trinity Street Cambridge CB2 3NG
Telephone 01223 568568
Email literature@heffers.co.uk

Lightning Source UK Ltd.
Milton Keynes UK
UKOW031304101111

181843UK00002B/2/P